The Urbana Free Library

To renew materials call
217-367-4057

THE AGE OF SINATRA

THE AGE OF SINATRA

A Novel
by
David Ohle

The Age of Sinatra
ISBN: 1-932360-32-8
©2004 by David Ohle

Cover Design by Charles Orr
ShortLit Series Design by David Janik and Charles Orr

Published by Soft Skull Press • www.softskull.com
Distributed by Publishers Group West • www.pgw.com

Printed in Canada

Library of Congress Cataloging-in-Publication Data

Ohle, David.
 The age of Sinatra : the sequel to the 1972 cult classic
Motorman / by David Ohle.
    p. cm.
 ISBN 1-932360-32-8 (pbk.: alk. paper)
 1. Titanic (Steamship)—Fiction. I. Title.
PS3565.H6A68 2004
813'.54—dc22
                    2004002999

They seem to have been strangely forgetful of the catastrophe.
—Plato, *Laws iii*

Only some hazy tradition about a conflagration of the world was repeated, without knowing how or when it occurred.
—Immanuel Velikovsky, *Worlds in Collision*

Portions of this novel, sometimes in different form, have appeared in the *Transatlantic Review*, the *Paris Review*, *A Reader of New American Fiction*, the *Missouri Review*, the *Dominion Review*, *Harper's*, the *Review of Contemporary Fiction*, *TriQuarterly*, *City Moon*, the *Pushcart Prize*, *Caliban*, *Conjunctions*, the *New Mexico Humanities Review*, and on the net at elimae, failbetter, and 3rdbed.com.

During the Age of Sinatra, just prior to the Forgetting of '64, an excavation near New Oleo unearthed a casket that, when opened, held a long-haired corpse encased in a wickerlike cage of overgrown fingernails. A metal name bracelet was found around the corpse's wrist, though rust and mold had obscured all but the middle name, which was Arvey.

AT FOUR BELLS, winded by the short walk from his cabin and bleeding from the nose, Moldenke was the first to arrive at the *Titanic's* deckside bistro, Der Kröetenkusser. Being early assured him of getting the outermost table, the one affording the best view of the promenade deck. The little table's metal top, however, was no larger than a dinner plate, and its spindly, uneven legs made tip-overs an ever present hazard. To the obsessively overcautious Moldenke, the table was something to keep a wary eye on.

Udo, the round-faced German barman, brought Moldenke a mug of fermented mulce, a tin of phosphate powder, a bowl of cubed fungu, and a small bale of smoking hair. "Hairloom brand, Moldenke. The best. By the way, how do you like the hand? Nice job, eh?"

The hand was cadaverous, blue, and all thumbs, the nails partly uprooted and seeping puss at the quick.

"Fine work. Who did it?"

"Dr. Ferry in New Oleo. If you're ever down that way, let Ferry work on you. You look so ordinary. You should have something done. What about those tiny ears? Wouldn't you like bigger ones? Different ones? Possibly from a French pig. Ferry's a pig man, you know."

Moldenke pulled a plug of hair from the bale and sniffed it. "I'll deform when they make it a law."

With his apron, Udo wiped leaking blood from one of the thumbs. "My uncle got a pair. He looks very sharp now, more streamlined. He's thinking of a third eye."

Moldenke indicated a ring of pinpoint scars around his mouth. "I'm a little shy of needles and knives. When I was ten, Mother sewed my lips shut with thick, black thread for spitting on her night-blooming jasmine. I couldn't eat, drink, or speak for three days, until my late, but kindly, father cut the thread with scissors."

He unzipped the front of his jumpsuit. "And this ugly, cruciform scar from nipple to nipple and neck to navel . . . four sheep's hearts went in there and a lung came out. My old ticker was failing."

"I'm impressed. But there's nothing like *elective* deformation. It's a different thing, a different feeling. You have to admit this is quite a hand. One-of-a-kind. A conversation piece. I'm having a special glove made."

"Here's a bit of conversation, Udo. This mulce stinks. Is it fresh?"

"Oh, yes. The first mug I've poured."

"You've boiled it to kill the tubularia?"

"For an hour."

"And the shigella?"

"Nothing could survive. Nothing. But add a lot of phosphate to be sure."

"Good. Now, please take that fungu away before I retch all over your clogs."

"Suit yourself. Some love it, some hate it. There's no in-between when it comes to fungu."

"Feed it to the gulls."

"I would, but they hate it."

Moldenke fluffed the hair with a tremor of the fingers and rolled a fat ciggie. "I thought the French had burned down the Hairloom factory and all the warehouses."

"They missed one on Permanganate Island."

"How fortunate. This smoke takes me to places where no word has ever entered, a place where nothing is comprehensible, nothing expressible. I'm quite addicted."

"Look at the time," Udo said, glancing at the sky. "Radio Ratt is on the air." He hurried to the bar and turned on his little radio. "You'd better listen, Moldenke. You know what they'll do if you don't."

This news from Radio Ratt: The president has indicated that his Bureau of Stinkers will discontinue reanimating the young. Those brought back thus far have had diminished mental capacity. One of the first to be returned, Little Jackie Dawes, wears a coat and helmet outfit of lightweight bulletproof chain mail, carries around a ragged mud-duck facsimile made of stuffed sox and pipe cleaners, and uses commodes built close to the floor so that his feet can touch the ground. Jackie sleeps the days away in a pillowed bathtub under a shade tree, a gourd of mulce resting on his fevered chest.

"A little Ratt goes a long way," Moldenke said. "Who elected him? When? We don't even know what he looks like."

"A runt," Udo said. "Shaped like a rutabaga I hear. Was there an election? I forgot."

Suddenly a wave of excitement washed across the deck. One of the ship's crew had spotted a dead plesiosaur in the water. Dozens watched the ship's davit haul the rotting hulk from a calm, gray sea in a rope basket.

"Another dead plesio," said Udo. "The one they fished up yesterday had a full-dressed American sailor inside, half digested."

A noisy sawfly encircled Moldenke's head again and again. He tried to bat it from the air with one hand, then the other, but his reach fell short each time. "Udo! Kill this flying lance before it pricks me."

Moldenke's mother had suffered a sawfly stinging once, on a summer outing, which sent her into a blind rage. Before it was over, she unmanned his poor infant brother, Andrew, with a pair of poultry shears and stuck his little scrotum on a picket fence. A few years later Andrew was trampled to death when the Pisstown Chaos spread to the countryside.

Udo took up the circular chase with a sturdy straw swatter. After smashing the sawfly on the wall, he fed it to a hungry, one-winged gull hopping around the bistro looking for spills.

By habit, Moldenke tugged lightly on his sparse chin beard, blinking one eye, then the other, but never the two at once, and added a spoonful of phosphate powder to his mulce, stirring it until thick foam spilled out of the mug and over the table top. With tremorous fingers he struck a damp, sputtering match, drew in all the smoke a single lung would allow, and let it seep out slowly through rotted teeth.

The plesiosaur caught his attention a second time when one of the ship's crew cut open its belly with a ditch blade and stepped back as hundreds of feet of intestine coiled into a steaming pile on the deck. When the stomach was located and opened, it yielded a slurry of half-digested junefish and sea slugs. The plesiosaur's neck, twenty meters long, supported a head of relatively minute proportions. There were four paddlelike limbs and a short tail. Its mouth was filled with a foul-smelling brown paste and its flesh hung like drying laundry from the bones.

When a sudden gust of wind swept the plesio's odor past Moldenke's nostrils, his arm twitched involuntarily, his elbow slid off the edge of the table, and he was thrown from his chair. His head struck the hard deck with the sharp *kunk* of a mallet pounding a peg. "Udo! Look at this table. You can't even lean on it!"

"Shush! Here comes the Captain," Udo said.

Holding his hat in front of his face, Captain Smith turned into the bistro with a slight gimp, his whites so heavily starched they rasped when he walked. He sat in the shadows at the far end of the bar, lit his hair pipe, and began reading a pre-edible copy of Ratt's *Manifesto*.

Radio Ratt:

Attacks on the French Camps will commence following the Congress of Neutrodynes . . . Judith Purdel, forewoman at Pisstown's Bloody Creek body mill, discovered the acid-soaked remains of Cumulus Crudders, a New Oleo Stinker, during an inspection. It is supposed Crudders had been substantially dissolved when the mill's containment vessel's skin was breached and spilled 10,000 aqueous tons of stomach acid, which came down with a tidal roar on the picnicking Crudders. . . . Charlotte Eng, neutrodyne Queen, will marry Vincent Goop, Secretary of Neutrodyne Affairs. Her dowry includes a bucket of frozen President Kenny semen and a neut-hair counterpane. Eng arrived by orbigator from Indiana today, her gold lamé tie flashing in the glacial sun. The marriage will be consummated after a feast of orchid-stuffed gibnut and hot raisin paste. The queen will ready herself for nuptials in the usual ways, tucking in her tulle, tending her hair, hanging her sash, douch-

ing, shaving, drowsing, eating sour mulce cheese, and grazing for other pleasures.

Udo, chopping green gland for the Captain's favorite soup, paused. "Look good, Moldenke. Here comes the ship's designated artist. Ferry did her leg work. Removed them, switched them, and put them back. The effect is beautiful, isn't it? No, it's sublime."

A faintly camphorated scent accompanied the artist's clumsy arrival at Moldenke's table. She carried a sketchpad under one arm and clutched a sizable bag of charcoal sticks. She had a tired, drawn look and a creamy, translucent complexion. There were flakes of dead skin caught like sleet in her eyebrows.

"May I?"

"Certainly. Have we met? I can't remember."

"We may have. I can't say. In the event we haven't, or we've forgotten, I'm Ophelia Balls."

"Moldenke, out of Indiana. Join me for a mulce." He accomplished a sliver of a smile without showing many teeth. "Careful of the table. It's a toddler. It loves to fall down and spill everything. By the way, that's a sweet-looking leg job."

Ophelia's jumpsuit, freshly starched and ironed, fit loosely on her skeletal frame. Above her long, black hair, soft forehead, and dreamy eyes sat a Vink thinking hat tilted rakishly to one side.

"Thank you."

"Ferry, I hear, did the legs."

"He's a wizard. Whatever you want, he'll do. I'm having trouble getting used to them, though. Always at the crossroads. The left wants to turn right and the right left."

Moldenke wiped blood from his upper lip with the back of his hand and pinched his nostrils closed. "Do I smell a Stinker in the area?"

"It's the plesio," Ophelia said. "I wish they would dispatch it."

"So many dead ones," Moldenke said. "Floating by all day."

"It's President Ratt, shooting them from his yacht. A disgrace. Haven't you read about it in the papers?" She began to sketch the dead plesiosaur.

"I don't read the papers. Something in the ink, perhaps. I break out in fulminant hives head to toe."

The tip of Moldenke's ciggie caught fire. He wet his thumb and a finger with mulce and dampened it. "This hair is fresh, it's moist, it's name brand, yet it wants to burn like dry leaves." He had a sip of mulce, then spit it back. "This needs more phosphate!" He added another spoonful.

Udo brought Ophelia a mulce. "With or without, ma'am?"

"Without."

"Don't be afraid of the foaming," Moldenke offered. "Phosphate's fertilizer for the brain. Besides, you never know what's living in there. . . . I see you're wearing a Vink thinker. Vintage, too."

"It's been in the family twenty or a hundred years. Possibly centuries. No one really remembers."

"You don't see Vinks much any more. I had one as a lad, but it went bad over time. Had to bury it in the garden and plant horseradish over it."

"This one's addled now, too, depending on the situation and the weather, but when it was new, it made Grandma Balls the smartest girl in Pisstown."

"Pisstown . . . Pisstown," Moldenke said. "I knew a Pisstown Balls. When I was driving one of those big pedal wagons right after the last Forgetting. I was running mulce and phosphate to the fusel oil camps. Roe Balls. His name was Roe Balls."

"A second cousin. The wagon overturned and a barrel of mulce fell on top of him. It burst and he drowned."

"So sorry to hear that. May he rest in peace." Moldenke bowed his head.

When Ophelia bowed hers, her Vink's soft pseudocranium moved molelike beneath the duck-cloth fabric. "Oh, my Vink just made a connection. Moldenke . . . Moldenke. I know that name. . . ."

"Agnes Moldenke, my mother. You've probably heard of her. She's quite well known."

"Of course, the inventor of edible money. Your mother?"

"Yes, she's aboard."

"I'm anxious to meet her. What's in the money? What's it made of? Can you tell me? I know it's a family secret, but—"

"It's never been disclosed, even to me."

"Where is it made?"

"That, too . . . is a well-guarded secret. And completely proprietary."

"When we meet, I'll try to pry it out of her?"

"I'm sure you will very soon. She's ill today, as she often is, and staying in her stateroom. The poor woman's been through an awful ordeal. She thought some time spent in the sea air would revive her spirits."

"Ordeal?"

"It can't be talked about. She doesn't remember. But the aftereffects never abate. Now it's a rather stubborn case of leukorrhea, accompanied by pinworms. The worms cause no end of trouble by their habit of coming out around the anus during sleep, leading to painful scratching and restless nights. She's able to remove them with a swab of cotton on an applicator rod. During this infestation she has been listless, anemic, and confined to bed, where she works on her memoirs whenever her strength permits. Well, as if that wasn't enough, just this morning, after completing the sentence 'Ink, is it not the blood of the diarist?' she ran the metallic point of the pen into her finger, making a small wound that bled dramatically. Some of the ink was drawn into the bloodstream, and that, she fears, could lead to infection. May I roll you a ciggie, Ophelia? Genuine Hairloom."

"Yes, I'd love one. But I thought the French had—"

"They overlooked a warehouse somewhere. It was on the radio."

"Oh, really."

Radio Ratt:

The great inventor Leuko Vink, vacationing at a Firecracker Sea resort, wants to put artificial suns and moons into orbit in order to illuminate parts of Indiana at night. These luminous bodies would permit nighttime harvesting, light up darkened polar regions, and disclose pockets of anti-Ratt activity in Indian Apple, Bloomberg, and other darkened Indiana cities. Vink has assured the President that there will be enough water produced by melting polar caps to turn the Tektite Desert green. The luminous bodies are described as "free-floating chemical furnaces." Fed by the oxygen-rich Indiana atmosphere, these glowing spheres of phosphate, radium, and fusel oil will burn for five to ten Forgettings. It is estimated that about three orbigators and eleven thousand neutrodynes would be needed to complete the massive task.

The *Titanic*'s horn sounded.

"Oh, dear," Ophelia said. "Time to praise Arvey. Just because Ratt worships at his altar, why should we be compelled to?"

Udo, placing another bale of hair on the table, said, "I've been warning Moldenke. Now I warn you, Miss Balls. Like it or not, Ratt rules. Think twice before you say these things publicly."

"I wonder if he even exists. He's all over the papers, he's on the radio, but has anyone ever seen him in the flesh?"

"Could be a fiction." Moldenke said. "The term 'president' may refer to a semiotic construct, just an idea, and not a person. How could we know? We've forgotten a lot."

"I've seen him," Udo said. "In the flesh. In Bum Bay, right in front of Neutrodyne Hall, getting into his pedal car."

Ophelia filled her mouth with smoke, drew it into her nostrils, and giggled. "They say he has the look of an amphibian."

"How good it was," Moldenke said, "when Sinatra and President Kenny were alive. It was a big country. So sparsely populated, a new face or a new arrival was reason for rejoicing. People turned their wagons inward and came together in the circle of firelight for safety. They cut down the forests, laid railroads, roofed barns, and husked corn."

"This is marvelous smoke," Ophelia said. "My Vink's telling me to talk about all my names."

"Go ahead," Moldenke said. "I'm all ears."

"I had a striking collection of them. After my parents' death, I was adopted in infancy by a neutrodyne couple, the Camulettes, who gave me the name Ophelia. When Camulette died, his widow turned me over to an American settler family by the name of Fallo, who changed my first name to Sally. This name I held until age thirteen, when the

Fallos died and I was taken in by an uncle of Mrs. Fallo, a Mr. Pester, who made me his heir and changed my name to Hester Pester—a ridiculous combination, I thought—so I induced the court to change my name to Wild Rose. But at the age of twenty, I married a German named Ochs, and although he pronounced it 'Oaks,' nearly everyone else called it 'Ox.' I was Wild Ox for as long as the marriage lasted, and until I married Mr. Balls, my brother, when I returned to my original name." She paused for another puff of smoke. "Excuse me for going on this way." She removed her Vink and stuffed it between her legs.

Moldenke asked if he could hold the Vink.

"Please, do."

He cradled it and rocked it back and forth. "You know," he said, "after smoking, an aura appears around my head— seen only at night and only in the deepest dark. Moreover, it throws the phosphate of potash from the top of my eye sockets. I find it on my face at bedtime. In order to keep well, given these precursors, I must have food containing phosphate to quickly and surely rebuild brain tissue. Fresh mulce is very good in this regard."

"I nearly married a neutrodyne once," Ophelia said, sigh-ing. "The wedding day stands out in my mind. Preparations had begun weeks before . . . brushing my body with mummy oil, dusting it with lavender. Following neutro-dyne marriage customs, I placed pads of linen in my eye sockets and shut the lids over them, so that they protruded unnaturally. It was the purest kind of joyous anticipation. But we would never marry. Billy was hanged on a spurious charge of defacing an Arvian temple by throwing excrement at its windows. Some local vagrants and tatterdemalions were guilty of the act, but all were in possession of waivers. Billy, worshiping in the temple at the time, was not. For many months he was sorely missed. I carved a small likeness of him from a knot of camphor wood and ended my virginity with it. I left it inside so that I would feel pain with every step and be reminded of my loss."

Radio Ratt:

After a ten-day sleep, from which physicians were unable to arouse her, former president Dorothy Peters has died from an ulcer of the stomach. In her last years, Peters, a widow, lived alone and in apparent harmony with a house full of gibnuts. "You could see dozens of them in the window," a neighbor reported. When a sergeant in charge surveyed the home in the beam of a lamp, bright red eyes peered back. On one occasion, the sergeant said, Peters opened the door and he saw gibnuts two or three feet long running around in filthy debris. Though dallying with gibnuts was in violation of the law, Peters possessed a valid waiver and the sergeant took no action.

"Time for vespers," Udo announced.

Shipwide, passengers, stewards, mates, all knelt and bowed their heads.

"I'd rather be hung with barbed wire than be subjected to this," Ophelia muttered. She remained standing.

The recitation began, a thousand voices raised against the roar of the sea. "We know not the hour, we know not the day, yet we watch and we wait, our lamps trimmed and burning. We watch and we wait for Arvey's returning."

When the horn sounded again, everyone resumed their activities.

"You should have knelt, Ophelia," Moldenke said. "You could get into trouble."

Udo stuck out his hand. "You stood out like one of these," he said, flexing the thumbs.

"Arvey this, Arvey that. I won't be a part of it. I refuse," she said.

"Don't say I didn't warn you," Udo said.

Radio Ratt:

In Bum Bay the propitiation of Stinkers has been a subject of much discord. The President issues the following directives: If a child spills mulce on the floor, say, "That's for the Stinkers"; if you throw slops out the window, cry out, "You Stinkers take care of that offal"; sew a small piece of iron into an infant's garment. A Stinker will never molest or colic that infant; fill a jar with pure stump water, add some honey, and place in the kitchen at night. The Stinkers, entering, will not touch the food in the cabinets, but content themselves lapping the sweet stump water; when checking out a Stinker, look at its shoes first, its eyes, nose, and teeth next. Never question a Stinker directly, or stare at it overlong. . . .

A tall, stoop-shouldered American approached the table hat in hand, a broad smile on his face, a parasol over his shoulder.

"Gerald Hilter. I write a column for the Bum Bay *Observer.* You may have read it. 'Hilter on the Seamy Side.'" He extended a hand that was far too heavy for its size and much too cool when shaken.

"Sorry, I don't read the paper," Moldenke said. "But, please, sit down and smoke hair with us. I'm Moldenke, of the Indiana Moldenkes." He rolled Hilter a ciggie. "When the moonlight falls upon the Wabash, I chill."

"I'm Ophelia Balls, artist, out of Pisstown."

"Oh, yes. I once wrote for the *Pisstown Telegraph.* Great little paper. Great little town."

"Here, Hilter," Moldenke said, holding the ciggie upright between two fingers. "Stoke up on some of this primo hair. It's contraband. Genuine Hairloom."

Hilter removed the beeswax plugs from his ears. "Just to keep the earworms out. They tell me the ship's infested." He had a strong pull on the hair. "Oh, my dear, this *is* very good smoke."

Moldenke, too, had a strong pull. "It's a puzzle how we even framed our thoughts before we had access to these lovely, fragrant, resin-scented vapors."

Ophelia said, "It gives you second sight. You finally understand the truth about things."

Taken with Ophelia's charm and good looks, Hilter tapped his parasol lightly on the toe of her clog. "If an inch were added to your height, my dear, you would be too tall. If an inch were taken away, you would be too short. Another grain of talcum and you'd be far too pale. A touch more of rouge would make you too red. But let me say this . . . I love those legs."

Moldenke pressed the Vink to his breast, then, with a regal sweep of his mug across the horizon, said, "All of history was a lie, all of science . . . everything." One of his eyes drifted from its focal point, then returned. "Documents lied . . . witnesses, governments, journalists, mothers, lovers, enemies, families, friends, religions, all lied." He returned the Vink to Ophelia, who stroked it to settle it down.

Hilter spat a little bloody curd onto the turtlewood deck. "Lungworms again," he said, blowing his nose into a handkerchief. "And look at this ball of whites in my hankie."

"Dr. Ferry's a real talent," Ophelia said. "Very competent. Good manner. They say he looked after Michael Ratt's scarlatina during the Pisstown Chaos."

Burping acidly, Moldenke said, "I've always had hope that someone, sometime, somewhere would mount *some* opposition to Ratt, but I don't see, hear, or smell any signs of it."

Hilter's long goatee rose and fell in a newly stirring breeze. "How can he lead us, inventing reality as he goes? A grand experiment is underway, I think. The grandest of all time."

Moldenke squeezed a piece of his wattle between thumb and forefinger. "And when the experiment is over, we'll be sacrificed, won't we? It isn't the dying that bothers me, it's that in precious little time, not only will I be gone, so too will be all memory of me. I will no longer even be referred to in conversation. I'll be *long* gone."

"What does it matter?" Hilter said, dragging on the ciggie. "When we have this lovely hair to smoke. Oh, I do think I'm approaching cricket consciousness. *Zeep zeep . . . zeeeeeeeeeeep.*"

Ophelia had another puff. "I died once," she said. "I was working as a toad eater for a charlatan and by accident swallowed a poison toad. My fever spiked, my brain boiled. I died, they say, technically speaking, although there was life. In a few days, I came back."

"*Zeep zeep.*"

Moldenke rolled the rest of the bale into ciggies. "What do you remember from the other side?"

"Time is more fluid, ever changing, ever elusive. You always stop just short of knowing exactly when. Who, what, and where, perhaps, but never when. Distances are great there, and fusel oil is in short supply."

"*Zzzzzzzzzzzzzz. Zzzz.*"

Udo raised the wick on his fusel oil lamp and busied himself slicing greasewood fruit with a sharp citrus knife and singing, "*Edelweiß, Edelweiß, du grüßt mich jeden*

Morgen, sehe ich dich, freue ich mich, und vergeß meine Sorgen. . . ."

The Captain stirred from his reading and sang along: "*Schmücke das Heimatland, schön und weiß, blühest wie die Sterne. Edelweiß, Edelweiß, ach, ich hab dich so gerne.*" A bowl of green gland soup and a foaming mulce sat untouched in front of him, attracting sawflies.

Radio Ratt:

A neutrodyne, Marcus Govinda, has given birth to a cross-breed from the mouth. Govinda exhausted doctors with a standing labor of nine days and nights. . . . Back in Indiana, Stinker actress Mitzi Gaynor has brought charges against the dancer and heiress, Sissy Peterbilt, whom she says assaulted her on a street in Indian Apple with a can of aerosol deformant. "Now I can only get monster roles," says Gaynor.

Moldenke's teeth ached, each in its characteristic way. They had begun to rot following his mother's lip-stitching assault. Even the cool air blowing across them when he opened his mouth was a minor agony. After rubbing hair ash on his bleeding gums, he spat into his palm and made the motions of hand washing. Then his eyes ran water. To clear them, rather than bring anything as unsanitary as a handkerchief or a sleeve in contact with them, he blinked one eye, then the next, never the two at once. The behavior was typical of the many forms of dyskinesia that plagued chronic hair smokers and phosphate addicts.

The Captain gulped his cooled soup from the bowl, rose abruptly, placed his hat in front of his face, and left. Though he slipped once on a gull squirt and nearly fell, he hurried along the promenade deck to his quarters.

"He's a lunarcentrist," Udo said. "Walks the deck at night when passengers are asleep. Takes measurements of the moon. That's the way he navigates."

"Pity us all," Moldenke said.

"More than that, I hear. He always has a dozen needles stuck through his scrotal bag, they say, in memory of a former inamorata. He wants to remember her with every step."

Radio Ratt:

In French Settlement Camp, a neutrodyne named Rocky has confessed that he found an American settler sleeping in a Pisstown shed, finished him off with a ball-peen hammer and swiped a pack of factory-made Hairloom ciggies from his top pocket. . . . Secretary of Neutrodyne Affairs, Vincent Goop, interrupted the monthly meeting of United Stinkers today, telling them that Stinker-neut couplings, soon to be outlawed, will be punishable by civil death. . . . And the latest from the Rattery are these words from the president: "This morning, near a school, I came upon a small settler boy spinning a top made from a gibnut's bladder. Remembering my childhood top-spinning, I offered to show the youth some helpful tricks. The boy put his top and grimy string into my hand and then watched wide-eyed as I spun the top faster and faster and faster as it was spanked by the string and coaxed to stay up in the air. A crowd gathered, and someone remarked, 'Mr. President, you didn't tell us about this talent,' to which I replied, 'It's time to let go of childish things. A new law will take effect at midnight tonight. No more top-spinning. Stop tops for a top-free world. Violators will be violated in ways I have not yet determined. Good night, people. May Arvey rest in peace and everything stay in balance.'"

As the afternoon faded hesitantly into twilight, Udo spotted one of the *Titanic*'s white-gloved sergeants strutting purposefully toward the bistro with a can of deformant in his hand. "Officer Montfaucon, and he's got a bead on you, Ophelia."

"I told you to kneel," Moldenke said.

Hilter shook his head. "This could be very bad. More than bad."

A heavily muscled veteran of the Pisstown Chaos, Montfaucon had lost an eye in that ambiguous scuffle, near the end of hostilities. Now he kept a gull's egg, changed daily, in the vacant socket. Other than protruding slightly, the egg fits well there, and benefited greatly from the incubation.

Montfaucon stood at rigid attention, the tip of his nose nearly touching Ophelia's. "Not kneeling for vespers, eh, Miss Balls? Brand new ordinance, just came down from the President. There's really no choice here. Appropriate punishment is very clearly prescribed. As soon as this ship reaches home port, you'll do some time in the French Sewer. Unless, of course, you have a waiver from the Ratt administration. And even if you do, I'm going to cover your face in this deformant."

"I do have a waiver." Ophelia produced a well-worn, well-folded, edible-paper form from the brim of her Vink thinker. "Here, Sergeant. This should take care of it."

Montfaucon examined the form. "It's old, but not quite expired. You still have one more free pass. My apologies, then. No punishment for you this time."

"Thank you, sir."

Montfaucon now stood nose to nose with Moldenke. "You. Do you have a waiver?"

"A waiver? Where do you get them? How do you—"

"No waiver?"

"But, Officer, I was kneeling. Everyone around here saw that."

"Yes, I know."

"Then . . . ?"

"Don't you read the papers?"

"He's referring to Ratt's new initiatives," Hilter said.

"Initiatives?"

"Share the guilt. Share the punishment," Montfaucon said. "Crime is not a failure of the individual, but of the culture. As long as *someone* is held accountable, and punished accordingly, that's jolly good for the commonweal."

"She goes free and I . . . ?"

"She has a waiver. And you do not."

"I'll get one. Are they available on board the ship?"

"From the purser."

"Simple enough, then. I'll go to the purser's right now."

"The office is closed, and will be until morning."

"I'll go then, in the morning. I suppose there'll be forms to fill out."

"Stacks of them."

"And the cost?"

"It changes day to day, person to person, sometimes dramatically. You make an appeal. The purser is the judge."

"Then let's be reasonable. I'll go to the purser first thing tomorrow and make my manners."

"I'm afraid not. Act like a man. What's the offender's name?"

"Ophelia Balls," Moldenke said. "She's standing right there."

The officer slammed his paddle against Moldenke's head. "You're the *official* offender, you idiot. What's your name?"

"Moldenke. Of the Indiana Moldenkes. You've probably heard of my mother, Agnes. She invented edible money.

I'm sure, with that kind of fame and prestige, a waiver can be . . . waived."

"You loathsome puke, hiding behind your mother's skirts."

Moldenke calmed himself by looking at the moon, gibbous and dull. "It's a bit red this evening," he said, hoping to mollify Montfaucon with casual, oblique talk. "A red moon, they say, makes it a good night for love . . . and mercy. Then, of course, when the moon is gray, they say, it's a good night for netting plesios."

Montfaucon farted, dry and vengeful, without odor. "The offender will now lower his jumpsuit and take ten, or twelve, until he is good and bloody."

Hilter peeled the pages of his notebook. "Sergeant . . . you don't mind if I make a few jottings here. I'm a columnist for the *Observer*. It seems to me that everyone should know about Ratt's new vision of crime and punishment. Don't you agree?"

"Indeed I do. Jot away. The Ratt administration, as we speak, is in full agreement with fair and truthful reporting."

Moldenke lowered his jumpsuit, shivered in the evening cool, and whimpered, "We know not the hour, we know not the day, yet we watch and we wait, our lamps trimmed and burning. We watch and we wait for Arvey's returning." The recitation emptied his lung. He gasped for breath, swallowing air like a fish.

"Stand up now. I'm going to squirt some deformant right into that pitiable face of yours."

"Stop this," Ophelia said. "Take my last waiver. Let him be."

"Gladly," Montfaucon said. "The way Ratt sees it, all pain rises from a single spring. Your pain is mine. Mine is yours. It's a cornerstone of his thinking. You may go about your business." He marched up the deck, stepping over the dead plesio.

Radio Ratt:

President Ratt was golfing with friends when a squall came up. For safety, they all gathered under the limbs of a camphor tree to wait it out. After a while the president left the others, saying, "I'm going to play the lie." He was striding toward the hazard when a z-shaped bolt landed, entering the crown of his head and exiting by way of the anus. His underwear was burned away and the spikes of his golf shoes melted. Physicians say he is alert, but has no recollection of the past. The amnesia is typical of such strikes, but temporary. . . . This from Point Blast on Permanganate Island. A new windblade was placed in service there today to disperse the seasonal necrotic winds that blow in from the southern waters. . . .

THE NEXT AFTERNOON Moldenke was again the first to arrive at Der Kröetenkusser. "Humiliating," he said. "I went to the purser's this morning. 'I'd like one of those waivers,' I say. He says, 'Sorry, Bub. The ink's still wet. Won't be dry till tomorrow.' I say, 'Fine. Please hold one aside for me.' He says, 'Can't do that. First come, first serve.' I say, "What time will you open?' He says, 'We're closed tomorrow. Ratt's declared a holiday.' 'A holiday?' I say. He says, 'It's his fifty or hundredth birthday. Big celebration in Dilly Plaza. No waivers issued on holidays.' Well, that was enough for me. I went to my cabin and sulked all day. I'll have a double mulce with plenty of phosphate and two bales of smoke."

"Brighten up, I have a surprise," Udo said. He positioned a Vink multismoker on Moldenke's table. "One of the ship's crew died last night, an oiler in the boiler room.

Asphyxiated himself. But I'm happy to say, just yesterday I won this from him in a game of Mexican dominoes." The hammered copper bowl and the colored glass chamber caught the glare of the setting sun. "Look there, Moldenke. Six smoking tubes."

Ophelia was the second to arrive at the bistro, each leg trying to steer her in a different direction. She gave her thinker a gentle nudge, as she sat down. It shook for a moment, then inflated.

Udo broke loose a handful from a fresh bale, balled it, filled the smoker, and lit it in several places. "This batch was cured in sucker weed sap. Good for the circulation, tonic for those old implants, Moldenke."

"Where the bee sucks, there suck I," Moldenke said, lifting one of the smoker's tubes and clamping his teeth on the stem.

"Oh, implants," Ophelia said. "That was the trend back then, before the Forgetting of '69, wasn't it?"

"Can't remember."

"What are they, the implants?"

"Sheep. Four of them. One's quit beating altogether. A second one is failing. My surgeon is aboard ship, oddly enough. Dr. Burnheart. We pass one another on the prom-enade, I nod, I smile. He acts as if I'm a complete stranger. The Forgetting hit him hard."

Ophelia's pencil roamed over a fresh sketchbook page, outlining what would become a caricature of Moldenke's long, slack-jawed face. "I was painting portraits of Stinkers on Holly Island when it struck," she said. "Just like that, everyone on the Island went completely blank. All except the Stinkers. Some of them could still recall the days when Kenny was president and Sinatra was singing. One of them claimed that Arvey killed Kenny. And that's when Ratt assumed office."

Moldenke rekindled the smoldering hair. "No, no. Dorothy Peters came after Kenny and before Ratt. Didn't she?"

"Who knows anymore."

"Smoke, Ophelia? It's very good. I'm already nearing cricket consciousness. *Zzzzzzzzzzzzzzzzzz. Reep, reep.*"

Ophelia clamped a tube between her teeth, applied her lips, and finished off the red-hot bowl. "Have you read Ratt's *Manifesto*?"

"Can't say I have. Or I don't remember."

"It's chilling in its simplicity. Everything should be kept in balance. There must be as much sorrow as joy . . . crime as punishment . . . pain as pleasure and birth as death. If these things get out of balance, another Chaos could occur."

"We were better off in the days when Sinatra sang, when happiness was not only considered achievable, but hailed as the ideal state of being. Now we scoff at the idea. So quaint, we think, to strive for happiness. For us it's a dead word."

Udo brought another bale of hair, a pitcher of mulce and a tray of boiled roots. "Three bales is the limit, now. I've dampened it for you, to make it burn slower. And here's some greasewood roots to chew on."

"Ophelia? Another ciggie?"

"One more and I'll want to lie in the grass, rub my knees together, and buzz."

Radio Ratt:

In Pisstown's buffer area, a French pig torch was started on a wild run by the explosion of a butter lamp, apparently the property of P. B. S. Pinchback, a neutrodyne born in Valdosta, who narrowly escaped burning to a cinder in his bed. Pinchback had gone to his room at eleven o'clock to retire. He lit the butter lamp, which caught fire within, and he threw it

into the street. The lamp struck the pig squarely in the middle
of the back and exploded, covering the animal with burning
butter. Its squeals rattled the sky. In a frenzy to avert the flames,
it wore about itself like a cloak, it set fire to the floor of a man
made insane by lightning ten years ago, Fate Perry, who was
sleeping above the Squat 'n' Gobble on Arden Boulevard.

Gerald Hilter, strolling on the deck, spotted Moldenke
and Ophelia. "Well, *bon soir*, may I join you?"

"*Mais oui*," Ophelia said.

"Smoke, Hilter?" Moldenke slid the smoker across
the table.

"Yes, please. I'm getting cloudy. I need a bump." Hilter
spat on the flaming hair to cool it. "I've been trying to mud-
dle through Ratt's *Manifesto*. If you ask me, it treats mean-
ing as artifact. No frame of reference. Utterly impenetrable."
His pale eyes closed momentarily, then opened, the lids
rolling up like window shades. He rested his heavy, lantern
jaw on the handle of his parasol. His chest inflated prodi-
giously as he filled his lungs. "Evolution's come to a stand-
still," he said. "There's precious little time left." He bit into
a root and chewed it gingerly. "Another Forgetting is on the
way. I feel it."

"We'll never make any progress, periodically forgetting
everything and starting over," Moldenke said. "Whatever is
gained in the remembering is lost in the Forgetting. It's one
step forward, two back."

Ophelia removed her Vink and dusted it. "What's so
wrong with forgetting everything once and awhile? I don't
mind tossing it all off, periodically beginning again with a
clean slate. There's only one primitive purpose to memory,
and that's to recognize old friends and enemies. If you *have*
no old friends or enemies, what's there to remember?"

DAVID OHLE

"And the Forgettings do tend to stir up a stagnant culture," Hilter said. "It's always undergoing rebirth and renewal that way. Ratt covers the subject extensively in the *Manifesto*, in the chapter on Contradiction. You live one lifetime, he says, but many lives, between Forgettings."

"Not a bad idea," Ophelia said.

"The newsroom is abuzz," Hilter whispered. "There's evidence now that it's the Radio Ratt broadcasts that bring on the Forgettings."

"It doesn't surprise me a bit," Moldenke said. "That's why they compel us to listen."

A neutrodyne entered the bistro, bringing about an abrupt change in the general mood.

"Look what's arrived," Moldenke said.

Hilter said, "For the President to declare us equal in abilities and dispositions with neutrodynes is an insult to natural intelligence. It's like saying razorbacks are as good as Durocs, or that a stump-broke mule is the equal of a thoroughbred. It doesn't stand to reason."

Udo scowled at the neut, who took a seat at the bar and said, "I'll have a double mulce with phosphate." Well-rooted to his chin and hanging down through an orange beard was a pendulous, fleshy sack that looked like a wurst in a butcher's window.

Moldenke averted his eyes. "He's got the biggest, ripest flocculus I've ever seen."

"My goodness," Ophelia said. "Let's hope he doesn't catch me staring."

The neutrodyne dumped a spoonful of phosphate into his mug, then giggled childishly as the mulce foamed over the top and formed a steaming green pool on the bar.

Hilter whispered, "He's looking at us. He wants to talk."

"Say there, Americans," said the neutrodyne, moving toward the crowded little table. "My apologies for the way I look. The name is Vink, son of the inventor. Yes, we neuts have no frame of reference, no cultural tradition. Yes, we decline the use of cosmetics. And we lack—"

"I'll tell you what you lack," Udo shouted from the bar. "You lack *luster*. You lack *élan vital,* you lack the complexity necessary to sustain the interest of your sympathizers."

"So go away and leave us to our modest pleasures," Hilter said.

"*Pourquoi, mon ami?* We're curious, friendly, intelligent. We take your behavior at face value and try to emulate it. It's the sincerest form of flattery, is it not? Why must you so consistently spurn us?" Vink's flocculus engorged, its baggy bottom sagging until it rested on the tabletop, sweeping aside a mug or two of mulce.

"I suggest we aim at a better understanding of one another," Ophelia said.

Hilter huffed. "Understanding? You can't be serious. They drift into public lavatories, poke through our stool with sticks, gaze at it through magnifying glasses, sniff it with the dedication of a *saucier* over his *Périgueux*. They sit beside us, feigning defecation. All to what end? It's beyond understanding."

Searching for a way to please his new acquaintances, Vink said, "Let me tell you a remarkable story regarding the heart of Louis the Fourteenth and how it came to be swallowed by the poet Blake. This was way before the Age of Sinatra. It seems that one day Blake was having his morning tea in a café in Lyons in the company of another émigré by the name of St. Dizier, when St. Dizier produced from his pocket something that looked like a piece of dried leather an inch or so long, which he presented to Blake. St. Dizier said, 'I was in the cathedral when the royal tombs were broken open and the contents scattered to the winds. This withered thing is the heart of Louis Quatorze, the Sun King. I managed to sneak away with it.' Blake wet the tip of his finger, rubbed it on the withered heart, then touched the finger to his tongue. 'Quite salty,' he said, and impulsively swallowed it."

"Go on," Ophelia encouraged the neut. "I love this. It's a good free show."

The neut said, "Last night I dreamed I was sitting cross-legged in a yard. In front of me was a featherless rooster in a pan of ice water. I was slapping it and spitting in its face. It was fiercely angry. A sergeant came along and arrested me, putting a blindfold over my eyes, slapping me, and spitting in my face. 'How do *you* like it!?' he demanded. I tried to explain that I was merely training my bird to be a fighting cock, but was nevertheless taken away to the lockup. The dream ended there."

Hilter scowled at the neut. "Please, go away. It's impolite to butt into other people's conversations the way you do."

"Fine, but before I go, let me tell you about a service I offer."

"Not interested," Hilter snapped.

"For only seven guida, you can piss in my beard. For five, in my face. On my flocculus, three. In the eyes and up the nose is two, and a combo of all those is eight."

"I've never tried this," Moldenke said, counting out seven guida and unzipping the fly of his jumpsuit. "Kneel down, Mr. Vink. My bladder's full as a tick."

The neutrodyne knelt in a prayerful attitude. "You Americans are a fun-loving bunch. Let me have it, friend. Soak me. Hose me down good and proper."

Moldenke aimed his flow in a sagging arc into the wiry beard.

"See how it drips from the bottom hairs," the neut said. "I like to look down and see that. It gives me quite a tickle."

PASSENGERS ENJOYED TWO days on Permanganate Island. Moldenke learned of a spa, famed for its medicinal baths, and went there. Greeted by the host, a short man with a strikingly large head and a lazy eye, Moldenke was quickly introduced to an array of clay cones, arising naturally from the soil, each about the size of a rain barrel. A soapy, purple mud gurgled from them, heavily charged with alkali, permanganate, and radium.

Moldenke was advised to disrobe and to squat inside one of the cones, where he drowsed away the entire morning buoyed up by the steady inrush of warm, irradiated mud. Afterward he was advised to step out of the cone and bake himself in the sun as other visitors to the spa were doing. Scattered about in mud cocoons, they looked like fallen statuary.

The host said, "We like our guests to mummy up a bit and let off steam. I'll return in a moment to break you loose with a pick and chisel."

A few days later, Moldenke was plagued by such ailments as rhinorrhea, emetic impulses, wens, hard knots, and kernels on the neck. He attributed these conditions to the effects of the radium.

ONE MORNING, ONLY a week or two out of Permanganate Island, as Moldenke breakfasted on mugwort tea and johnnycakes, he was informed by Del Piombo, the *Titanic*'s sergeant in charge of security, that the Captain had been murdered in the night. "Someone forced entry to his quarters, rinsed his mustache with chloroform, beat him viciously, pierced his heart with a darning needle, scissored off an ear, had a bowel movement on his puce carpet, then enjoyed a bath in his tub. Most extraordinary of all, a small red bean was sprouting from the Captain's ear. For this I have no explanation, unless it was carried there by an earworm and sprouted in the wax, which I observed to be redolent and abundant."

Piombo invited Moldenke and a few other passengers to attend the postmortem, to be conducted after a plaster likeness was taken of the Captain's face.

"A face I've never clearly seen," Moldenke said.

"Always the hat," said Piombo, and led them to a makeshift morgue below deck where the Captain's corpse, slit open, had been set atop a row of wooden casks, the hat sitting on his face. Ophelia was on the scene, a patch of angry blisters on her forehead, making sketches as Dr. Burnheart aspirated fluids from the Captain's chest cavity with a sharply pointed surgical instrument.

"Step closer," he said. "I'll show you his face." He lifted the hat.

Ophelia turned to a fresh page in her sketchbook. Her hands were unsteady and she dropped the charcoal more than once. Each time she did, she crushed it underfoot and continued with a new stick.

The Captain's face was unremarkable in all ways but one—on his chin was a mound of bruised flesh with an opening on the end that leaked a pale yellow fluid.

"It looks like a little volcano," Burnheart said. "It's what he's been covering. This is the very first case I've seen. Without doubt, this disturbing lump is the beginning of a flocculus. Until now, I would have said they were not transferable from neut to human."

Moldenke said. "His cabin boy was a neut. Had a flocculus, too."

"All the more reason," Burnheart said. "I would caution everyone here: keep your distance from neuts who have them."

"We'll hang the cabin boy," Piombo said.

"He has a waiver," Moldenke said. "I saw him displaying it proudly outside the purser's."

After removing the Captain's liver, Dr. Burnheart held it aloft, stared curiously at it, placed it in a pan of brine, then razored open the scalp and peeled it back. Moldenke took great pleasure in seeing this and a drop or two of semen wet his underdrawers.

THE FOLLOWING DAY the Captain was buried at sea with a minimum of ceremony. A small crowd of mourners gathered under parasols and Ophelia read from the works of Byron: "Roll on, thou deep and dark blue ocean,—roll! ten thousand fleets sweep over thee in vain; man marks the earth with ruin . . ." Here the Captain's muslin-wound body was flung over the rail, his hat spinning and sailing on the air behind him. ". . . he sinks into thy depths with bubbling groan, without a grave, unknell'd, uncoffin'd . . . and unknown."

THREE DAYS LATER, as dinner progressed, neutrodynes aboard ship dressed in ragman costumes, played brass instruments, their flambeaux burning, and marched from the late Captain's quarters to the upper deck and back down again, assembling on the mezzanine above the bistro, where they prepared to hang a two-headed neut, Darby Shushan, an innocent kitchen worker sentenced to die for the Captain's murder.

Moldenke, his mother, and Gerald Hilter watched these doings from Der Kröetenkusser as they enjoyed a meal of baked plesio, terrine of mud duck, and shredded root salad.

"Piombo wasted no time on this case," said Mrs. Moldenke.

Moldenke said, "We should be grateful it's Darby up there. Piombo could have pinned this on anyone. They'll just hang that stupid neut and that will be that."

"Let's be fair," Ophelia said. "Some of the neutrodyne ideas are a little unformed. But I do think they have a few good ones, too."

Moldenke smirked. "Name them . . . name them."

"For one, the months of their lovely calendar: Vintage, Fog, Sleet, Snow, Rain, Wind, Seed, Blossom, Pasture, Harvest, Heat, and Fruiting."

"They stole it from the French," Moldenke said.

"Occasionally, you'll find a neut who's adept at business," Mrs. Moldenke said. "And business has always been the art of making guida."

"Mother should know. Mother, the tycoon."

Mrs. Moldenke's full bosoms shifted leftward with a *swoosh* of undergarments as she raised her hand to point a finger at Moldenke. "Remember, my boy, children who play with modeling clay grow up to be tycoons. Art is the manipulation of a medium, any medium. Business is the manipulation of the medium of currency."

"See," Moldenke said. "This old woman knows her business."

"I do indeed."

"And such forward-looking ideas."

"I strongly urge marriage among siblings. You'd always have a pretty good race that way."

"She spent great energy urging me to perform coitus with my sister, Hetty," Moldenke said, "though I never did. She intended to take the offspring and raise it as a house servant, schooled from birth to care for her in her dotage."

"What gives me my energy," Mrs. Moldenke said, "is that I drink a liter of lithia water before bedtime, which I find excellent for renal calculi and all diseases dependent on a uric acid diathesis."

"Not to change the subject," Hilter said, "but shouldn't we be addressing the issue of the President's new directives?"

"I loathe Ratt and all he stands for," said Mrs. Moldenke. Using both hands, she lifted one of her bosoms and held it in a basket formed by intertwined fingers. "I quite clearly remember his Big Shift. An awful time. From the comfortable confines of my Holly Island summer home, I was obliged to catch the midnight pedal train to Pisstown, where I lived in virtual slavery with a horrible, brutal, burn-scarred veteran of the Chaos, for a period of many months, until I was shifted again."

"And I," said Hilter, "was not shifted, but forced to house shiftees in my small apartment, as many as a dozen at a time, including motherless children. It was asses and elbows and wailing all night."

Darby Shushan was brought to the gallows. The hangman applied the rope, slid the knot until it touched the napes of the two necks. Then followed the results of unequal ropes, an unfortunate oversight, which left one head alive fully thirteen minutes longer than the other. The living head made use of the time in a practical way, by mimicking birds with quite a repertory of warble and chirp, and singing maritime ditties. To finish him, the unfortunate neut had to be tugged and pulled at until a death egg came forth from the anal part in a gush of cloudy plasma. A French settler bent over and gathered it into his oilcloth hat. "*Aha, les oeufs de mort, pour les enfants,*" he said, puncturing the egg with a nail, then going around among the gathered children, giving each a taste of the tarry, sweet black yolk.

WHEN AGNES MOLDENKE was eighteen she attended the Dorothy Peters Institute in Bum Bay and solved the problem of school expenses by constructing her own portable home at the edge of campus. It consisted of a pedal wagon built on an old pre-Forgetting auto chassis, the wooden sides being covered with a canvas roof. Inside there was a bunk, a stove, a table, a chair, and a rack for books. She managed to live on very little by doing her own housekeeping and eating only crickets and johnnycakes. If one visits the Institute, even today, one can see her cozy wagon, reconstructed in painstaking detail, down to the chamber pot and its darkly waxen contents.

Radio Ratt:

A Stinker mother wept in Dilly Plaza's Eternity Meadows today, as her unknown son was disinterred. Later, the son's unknown sisters reburied the body in a brown bag. The large mother, shrouded in a drab cloth, swaddled the child's head closely, oblivious to the Arvian pickets who had come to hector, jeer, and spit. The father of the unknown son has eluded the law for years by living in distant Indiana. It was thought his son's disinterment might bring him out of obscurity. But it did not. For income, this Stinker mother receives edible money and loose change under the door for small favors. After the birth, the mother's friends and sympathizers had dropped off, and the cir-

cle of those who did not know her gradually enlarged. "I felt myself disappearing," the mother said, "in little pieces. If I became known again, I would be a nonentity. I do not exist." Three of the mother's other unknown sons and ten of her daughters survive. . . . Campaigning in New Oleo, President Ratt disclosed plans to revise the arithmetic. "It makes sense," he told the press. "Forty, fifty, sixty, seventy, eighty, and ninety each signifies a certain number of tens. This is scientifically correct, but the numerals from ten to twenty are named after a different method and the irregularity is inharmonious, confusing, and completely out of balance. Eleven, which is really ten and one, should be expressed by the name onety-one. The number twelve should be changed to onety-two. Then should follow onety-three, onety-four, onety-five, and so forth until twenty, which would be expressed as two-tens."

THE FRENCHMAN, TOPINARD, who collected prodigies, invited interested parties to the *Titanic*'s library for a get-acquainted session with his two neutrodyne giants, Indole and Skatole. Both male, both standing just over nine feet, they were being taken to Bum Bay for exhibition purposes.

While Indole was dressed plainly in a black hopcloth suit and handmade clogs, Skatole wore on his breast numerous exquisite nickel-plated pectorals and various amulets arranged in sixteen layers. Some of the pectorals displayed elaborate cloisonné work.

Ophelia sketched with easy, gracious strokes of the charcoal. "They burn neut bones to make this charcoal," she said. "It's the finest available."

Hilter went around opening portholes. "Please, a little air, if you don't mind, Mr. Topinard."

DAVID OHLE

Topinard, a thin wisp of a man, sat between his giants atop three or four edible editions of Michael Ratt's *Manifesto*. "They do offend," he said.

Moldenke peeled a scabby patch of dead skin from his scalp, discreetly dropping it to the floor and covering it with one of his clogs. "Amen to that," he said.

After latecomers were seated, Topinard's session began. "As a rule, these big beasts are liars in proportion to their height. They are indolent, unamiable, irascible, asocial, extremely talkative, and unpleasant to live with. They will not stay in private rooms and they wander about at night, never letting you sleep."

Moldenke executed an irregular but recognizable smoke ring. "You wouldn't keep such a wife."

"And no wife would suffer a husband like that," Hilter added.

"What about sexing?" Ophelia asked.

"Skatole, let them have a look at your member."

Skatole unbuckled his wide canvas belt and let the trousers tumble into a foul-smelling mound.

"Surprising, isn't it," Topinard said, "when you consider the size of the other parts, what modest reproductive organs my big neuts have. Fortunate, too, as this one has so far married three neut females of average height and fathered, in all, twelve young. Had the organ been proportionate, I'm afraid his life might have been a wreckage. You see, among neutrodynes, gian*tesses* are in critically short supply. Always have been."

"Can they speak well?" Hilter asked.

"Oh, yes. *Oui. Certainement.* They came through the last Forgetting with their wits about them. Say something, Skatole, for the people. Mind you, he speaks in some pre-Forgetting English dialect no one remembers."

The giant hiked his trousers and sat down. Even sitting, he had to bow under the low ceiling and let his flocculus rest on the floor. "John Lennon em I wanpela biknem tru long taim yu harim singsing bilong ol Beatles o Binatang. Long Mande nait long taim em wantaim meri belong em Yoko Ono I kam bek long haus bilong tupela long Nu Yok, wanpela man I sutim em long gan. John I gat 40 krismas. Ol I kisim em kwiktaim i go long wanpela haus sik tasol tarangu indai pinis. Na ol plisman I holim pasim wanpela man Hawaii pinis. Em i Mark David Chapman. Ol plis I tok, John Lennon I bin sainim nem bilong em long buk bilong dispela kilman long apinum—"

"That's enough, Skatole. You see, complete jibberish. A forgotten tongue. No one has a clue to what it all means."

"He seems agitated," Hilter said. "Is he high strung?"

"It unnerves him that we don't understand his strange blather. I often find him crouched in a corner, weeping and eating his feces. He's a dedicated coprophage, an unusual condition among big neuts. This, too, adds another dimension to his volatile nature. By far the safest and best work I have found for Skatole is moving his and Indole's manure in a wheelbarrow. I'd say, together, the two generate about a barrelful in a day. He can perform this work in the open air and at an easy, go-as-you-please pace. Working alone, and with an implement that cannot be turned to harm, he is in little or no danger of being imposed upon, driven too hard, or injured by others. I do have to stand by and keep them from eating too much of it, though, before they get to the compost."

"Let's hear from Indole," Moldenke suggested.

"Indole, show them how smart you are."

The light weight of Indole's flocculus, modest, unripe, all but hidden in his great black beard, permitted him to hold his head high as he spoke. "Alexander the Great, seeing Diogenes looking attentively at a pile of human bones, asked the philosopher what he was looking for. 'That which I cannot find,' was the reply. 'The difference between your father's bones and those of his slaves.' Shall I go on, Mr. Topinard?"

"*Oui*, more."

"*Bien Monsieur*. . . . According to *The Encyclopedia of Witchcraft and Demonology*, witches rubbed themselves with an ointment to facilitate flying. While the ingredients of this ointment varied from place to place and from time to time, there were four that were considered essential: a thick stew of children's corpses, preferably unbaptized, and the juices of henbane, wolfsbane and cinquefoil—"

Indole paused for a breath or two, then continued. "There are eight kinds of witches: one, the diviner, Gypsy or fortune-telling witch; two, the astrologian, star-gazing, planetary, prognosticating witch; three, the chanting, canting, or calculating witch; four, the veneficial or poisoning witch; five, the exorcist or conjuring witch; six, the gastronomic witch; seven the magical, speculating, sciental, or arted witch; and eight, the necromancer."

Without knowing why, Moldenke was suddenly beset with contradictory impulses and unusual urges. He excused himself, quietly left the library, and walked the deck to relax. Glad to see the light on in the ship's pharmacy, he sought the druggist's advice.

"Come in, Moldenke. You look blanched. What is it, unlawful impulses?"

"You've hit the nail on the head, Dick."

"Let me show you something." From a waist-level drawer whose pulls were badly worn with long use, Dick snatched a drawstring sack. "This goes for twoty-eight zil. Basically, it's a nice soft bag made from the scrotal sack of a well-aged neut. And inside, this." He withdrew a lash in which thorns, needles, and greasewood burrs had been woven.

Seeing the lash released a memory from Moldenke's Indiana past. As an adolescent, his passion for neutrodyne females had been something quite unmanageable. His monkish tendencies ever in conflict with his savagery, he became emotionally encysted and sought relief in passive sexual congress with them. He undressed in concealed places and paid them to lash him until his shoulders and buttocks bled. After such indulgences, his hands fisted, were cold, and wouldn't open. Hives showed themselves on his back and face. He scratched and raked at them continuously, then rubbed his thumb and forefinger together below his nostrils, as if in sniffing the dander he might intuit a remedy.

"This set has sold very well ever since they outlawed sexing with neuts," Dick said. "I really don't understand what it's all about, but it has to do with Ratt's pain and pleasure principle. The use of this, as instructed—it comes with written instructions—will help to keep things in balance. You should do your part."

"All right, Dick."

"You *will* be voting for Ratt, won't you?"

Moldenke crossed his fingers. "I will if you are."

"It's not good to be sitting on the fence in times like these."

"It certainly isn't."

"They say there's a plan to kill him. To kill Ratt."

"If he exists at all."

"Beg pardon?"

"Some people wonder if he even exists. So I hear anyway. Not that I think he's anything but solid and real. It's probably a rumor. Good night, Dick."

Once in the privacy of his cabin, Moldenke removed his clothes, knelt on the floor, and dragged the lash repeatedly between his legs, moaning with pain. He closed his eyes and brought forth images of the complex, pleasingly shaped pudenda of young neutrodyne females, which filled him with pleasure.

As he lay abed later, still bleeding in places, it occurred to him that, indeed, some sort of balance had been brought about by the self-imposed lashing. He was at peace with himself, the strange urgings and impulses becalmed. Was it within the realm of possibility that Ratt was right? That he was more a visionary than an idiot? If, of course, he existed at all.

Radio Ratt:

An American troublemaker living on the margin of the Fertile Crescent dynamited the antiquity known as The Living Rock, which has attracted thousands to the Crescent with its charming carvings of pre-Forgetting bears, wolves, serpents, and, strangest of all, a kangaroo. The Living Rock once towered on a corner of the property of the unidentified American, but now lies like a pile of eggshells on a compost heap. The American will be tried today, sentenced tomorrow, and Friday will hang.

MOLDENKE SUFFERED GREATLY in the deadening stillness as the ship entered the quiet waters off the Fertile Crescent and a dank, miserable envelope of bad air surrounded the ship day and night. A victim of *ejaculatio praecox*, Moldenke had nightly dreams that ended in pollution. His semen had a peculiar consistency and when he masturbated there was a severe cramp in the femoral region simultaneously with the orgasm. Only a small drop came, but afterward, while he was washing, the real semen flowed, as insubstantial and watery as skimmed mulce. He feared he would never father children.

AFTER A SLEEPLESS night, Moldenke walked the deck at dawn. His faith in Nature's order was shaken when he found a small toad in the ship's rain gauge. It was destitute of a head and had begun to putrefy. How it came to be there he could not imagine, unless it fell from the sky. Then he saw that the decks were covered with small masses of jelly, each about as large as a horsebean. He carried one of these to Dr. Burnheart, who examined it microscopically and said, "Yes, what we have here is *sputum lunae*, literally moon spit, sometimes known as sperm astrale, or star semen, thought to be an efflux of the moon. These lumps often fall from the sky, and sometimes prove to contain the ova of insects and worms."

On another morning stroll, outside the purser's, he witnessed Topinard punishing Skatole for some offense. "*Cochon!*"—"Pig" he exploded, a vicious stamp of heavy-soled shoes on the giant's toes emphasizing his invective. Again and again the shoes descended with violent impact.

Skatole crouched, trying to avert what blows he could. But his face showed great welts, and one lip, cut and bruised, began swelling. The blood ran in a thin cascade from above his right eye and fell upon the deck in great drops, which he smeared with a bare foot.

Skatole cried out, "Na bihain liklik ol I lukim wanpela man I wok long wokabaut raunin haus bilong John."

Topinard pruned his lips with annoyance and kicked the giant in his shin. "Stop your blather, man! Please! I'm going mad with it." He washed the giant's tongue with fatted soap and a scrub brush. "Time and again I have warned you. Do not speak until spoken to."

Skatole sank to his knees and wept.

Not far off, Indole stared directly into the blinding light of the risen sun, his eyes cast over with a chalky film.

"Why do you do this?" Moldenke asked.

"I want to be blind. This will hurry the process."

"Good morning, Moldenke," Topinard said, smashing Skatole's toes a final time, then extracting a coiled hair two feet long from a pustule on Indole's chin by popping it with a lit ciggie. "We'll be out of these doldrums as soon as tomorrow, I hear on the radio."

"Good morning, Monsieur. My mother says she'll have a go at stirring up some wind. She knows the ways. And I think I'll have a go at getting a waiver as long as I'm here at the purser's. The office should open any minute."

"I hate bearing bad news, but the purser is dead, possibly a suicide. He was a careless smoker with a long history of accidentally burning his clothes and household goods. One of the health problems causing his depression was extremely malodorous flatulence arising from abdominal surgery. He had a history of striking matches in the belief that the burning sulfur ameliorated the unpleasant odor. The fire investigation revealed the purser was sitting on the pot when his clothing caught fire. He was wearing pajamas with the pants in place at the waist. Burned matches were on the floor. There was evidence the fire started in the crotch area of the pajamas."

Moldenke said, "It seems unlikely that anyone would select this bizarre vehicle for suicide over less painful and more certain means. And, speaking of certainties . . . I won't be getting a waiver today, will I?"

"Not the smallest chance," Topinard said. "It's time for me to put these fellows to sleep. They've been up all night. They don't like the stillness any better than we do."

Toward evening, Mrs. Moldenke gathered passengers for a rally. They formed a tight circle around her and she said, "Now we're going to raise the sky with our voices and stir up the south wind. Let's go . . . altogether now. Yaaaaaahhhhh . . . hoooooooo. . . . Yaaa . . . hoo!"

The others joined in and shouted *"Yahoo"* for a time and then fell silent to listen. A groan could be heard from the sea bottom. The *Titanic* rose on a massive swell and the groan repeated itself, this time a good bit louder. The spray in the passengers' faces was warm, the surface of the water getting ever steamier, as if it would soon boil.

"It's the sound of subterranean strata readjusting themselves," Mrs. Moldenke said. "I think we've dislocated them. We should stop now. The sky is already rising. The winds should begin to stir."

EXCLUSIVE TO THE *Observer*.

The Agnes Moldenke Interview

G.H. Is it true, about the glue?

A.M. No one could leave a bottle of mucilage around the Moldenke home. It drove me into a frenzy and I would not be satisfied until someone took off the rubber nipple and poured the sticky stuff down my throat.

G.H. Where does that incredible endurance come from?

A.M. As a youngster I hardened myself by undertaking stringent diets and going around naked to the waist when others wore thick, padded overcoats. On Holly Island, I took to wearing a lock of hair on my forehead and had my portrait painted a number of times in Bonaparte's famous pose.

G.H. Always retaining that youthful figure.

A.M. For a time I took to wearing one of inventor Vink's La Grecque Reduction Belts whenever I went dancing. Made of radium pellets encased in the purest Para rubber, the device carried fatty exudations out of my body and into a rubber drain bag at a hidden location in my clothing.

G.H. Fascinating. They say you were an endocrine casualty.

A.M. During the Pisstown Chaos I was clubbed in the head by a raging neutrodyne. I became a violent-tempered and selfish paraphiliac. A prickly feeling went through me, a voluptuous pleasure, when animals were beaten in my presence, or if I read tales of cruelty, about torture, the rack, or the gallows.

G.H. And all the surgeries, one after the other, the scar scarcely healed over before you were sliced open again. Which stands out in memory?

A.M. Many years ago, when I had begun to turn yellow, surgeons removed a ten-pound teratoma from my uterus. In it were the small brown teeth, shriveled testes, and knotted hair of an unborn brother, either of mine or my son's. It was never determined.

G.H. Your son tells the story of the beetles in a matchbox.

A.M. He once presented me with some beetles he'd collected. I slid the box open and daintily bit each of the insects in a way that would immobilize but not kill immediately. Then I put them in a pile on the carpet and watched them slither, agonize, and twitch. When they were dead, I ate them.

G.H. The terrapins. What about the terrapins?

A.M. Once, in the month of Blossom and before the last Forgetting, I was engaged in clearing out a body of marsh land on one of my properties when I came across a den of terrapins. I lined a wooden box with damp neut hair. The terrapins were laid in rows on the cotton and covered with another hair layer. On top of this was placed a second row of terrapins, and so on, until the box was filled. The box was then covered with a blanket and stored in the cellar. There the terrapins slept through the winter while, upstairs, huddled near my stove, I illustrated *The Story of Edible Money* and wrote my enduring masterpiece, *The Book of Surprises*.

G.H. We know you use neutrodyne labor in your money mills, but your relations with them have always been strained. Why is that?

A.M. My son and I were sleeping soundly together about five o'clock one morning when a neutrodyne male wearing ornamental headgear and a nightshirt appeared at the bedside and had one foot in the bed when I woke up and screamed. But the intruder merely grinned and then lay down, pulling up the quilts and preparing to sleep. My son grabbed the lunatic neut and tried to gain mastery by holding him to the floor, but he struggled free and and wiggled off into the kitchen, shortly returning with an empty molasses tin, which he slammed over my head before running off at breakneck speed. A rim on the inside of the can sliced my tongue and wedged behind the gum.

G.H. Your son then ran to the shed and—

A.M. Got a pair of tin snips to remove the can, but when that proved too dangerous, glycerine was applied and the tin came off easily. Only the tip of my tongue was lost, falling into the carpet pile, never to be found. Then, of course, when I was visiting New Oleo, I was hit in the face with some acid thrown from the rear window of an Arvian church. I slipped to the pavement, impeded by a loss of vision. When I called out for assistance, a neutrodyne rushed from the church sacristy, bathed my eyes with violet water, and dabbed them with unguent. When questioned, the neut said, "I was only taking lacquer from an old parson's bench and threw the used-up acid out the window. How could I have known that such a personage as Mrs. Moldenke might choose that moment to walk by?" So, you see, my feelings are mixed. As Ratt says, all things in balance.

G.H. The bad neut harms, the good neut heals. A perfect balance. So then, in addition to your son, you had a daughter, Hetty. Tell us that story. Technically, she was dead, but you brought her back for awhile.

A.M. I taught Hetty to speak in a straightaway and truthful fashion, mimicking the journalese of late Americana. Hetty died one burning hot day when she gave up trying to cool off with lemonade and a bamboo fan and hopped into an old icebox in a fatal effort to lower her body temperature. She was clever enough to prop the door open with a stick, but a sudden gust of wind blew across the French-occupied valley and carried the stick away, slamming the door. Hetty appeared lifelike and normal after death, pliable of skin and ruddy cheeked, not entirely gone.

G.H. The carriage of death had indeed stopped for her, but she hadn't climbed on.

A.M. Burial hardly seemed proper. So I kept Hetty in the sunroom for many years and gave her a fine corduroy sofa to lie on. Her corpse was a good barometer, the belly swelling at any rise in atmospheric pressure, thus forewarning of dangerous storms, and deflating when fair weather prevailed. Her hair continued to grow on a regular schedule and had to be cut every so often. The tear ducts likewise remained active, oozing a cloudy lymph every solstice, and pungent gases often jetted from her anus. Under a compulsion that began just prior to the Chaos, I began collecting Hetty's exuviae—saliva, tears, stool, ear wax, dandruff, vaginal discharges, nasal crusts, and fingernail clippings—in airtight jars, labeled by year, day, and hour. These jars I stored in the attic, right next to the sucker weed tonic.

G.H. What, exactly, did you do to bring her back?

A.M. I made her breathe the fumes of boiling camphor oil and ingest acidophilus. First thing each morning she drank her own urine, still warm. I performed moxibustion on her, burning dry moss in little glass jars, then setting them at various strategic places on her body. The heated air made the jars suck at her flesh like leeches, leaving painful red welts, particularly in the cup behind her knees and the outer ankle—both places thought to be important in stimulating the bone marrow and the production of white blood cells. Her chest and abdomen were covered with healed-over lesions and her flesh resembled clay. If I grasped a handful of loose abdominal flesh and pulled it outward, the lobe of skin sagged in place like a doughy breast and remained that way several days, gradually shrinking back. I then conducted a macabre experiment in an effort to improve her digestion. I cooked one gibnut and fed it to nineteen other gibnuts. Then I fed one of the nineteen to the remaining eighteen, and so on, until only one was left. That one I stewed in mulce and blood and fed to Hetty."

G.H. Her fiery adolescent temper led to legal complications, later, and you intervened.

A.M. In the later part of '68, just before . . . or after . . . I forget . . . that first big Forgetting, I found work for Hetty at an upholstering firm. A clumsy neutrodyne worker by the name of Cirella dropped a piece of Hetty's duck cloth on the floor and Hetty hurled a heavy pair of carpet shears at her, severing her flocculus at the root. The neut bled until the end of the day and died when the sun went down. I settled a fair sum on Cirella's family and, by using my civic influence, fixed Hetty's stay in the lockup at a merciful week. In her cell, which was the breeziest and most comfortable in the jail, she was provided nightly meals of johnnycakes, greasewood roots, and green gland stew, while her cap, umbrella, and cane were left hanging close at hand. To amuse herself, she gave fellow prisoners charts of their phrenological traits. When that bored her, she trifled with learning to fiddle.

G.H. Then you lost her a second time.

A.M. Back in Indiana, Hetty was picking camphor berries and standing on a ladder when a French pig entered the yard. Naturally the dog gave chase, bumping the ladder and throwing her to the ground, fracturing both her thumbs. Three days later, the monad of tetanus invaded her body and she grew comatose. Realizing the hopelessness of the case, I turned to the bee sting. I removed her clothing and strapped her to an old hickory stump. After lathering her face, throat, breasts and scalp with honey, I retired to the house. The bees soon came in great numbers, stinging her many times, so that her head was swollen twice its normal size and her budding breasts looked like strawberry tortes. But the cure was effective. In a few days she was well enough to bake macaroons and say her daily prayers. She'd become an Arvian, against my wishes.

G.H. Ma'am, do I hear in that a hint of anti-Arvey senti-ment?"

A.M. Excuse, please, but I've got to make for the pot. I'm gassed up and cramping.

G.H. Sorry we have to end this so abruptly, but thank you so much, my dear Mrs. Moldenke.

A STRONG WIND suddenly rose from the south just as Mrs. Moldenke trundled toward the pharmacy, something of an uphill climb as the ship angled over swells. When she entered, hoping to find a good stock of charcoal tablets, she found Dick half-conscious on the floor, spitting up blood. Dr. Burnheart was attending him. "I'm afraid old Dick here's eaten some rat bait. He's been despondent in recent days. All we can do is try to make him comfortable. I've already had him swallow Ipecac, hoping to induce regurgitation."

When Dick vomited everything he could, and while Mrs. Moldenke waited impatiently, Dr. Burnheart pronounced the danger largely over, advised a night's sleep and a moxibustion treatment in the morning.

"I've been cabinbound two weeks," Dick gasped. "Failing to break wind when pressure was felt, living in fear of diverticulitis, forgetting to take enteric precautions."

"I'm suggesting," said Dr. Burnheart, "that this sort of severe malaise is an effect of the dying of the wind. Now that the southerlies have commenced, we'll all feel a lot better."

"Meanwhile, I'll just clench up and strive," Dick said, sitting up. "What would you like, Mrs. Moldenke? You look a trifle bilious."

"A bottle of aquafoenic, please, and a tin of charcoal tablets."

Dr. Burnheart helped Dick to his feet. "All I've got left is mummy powder. Mix it into a cup of mulce and there you are. Big shortage of charcoal tablets."

A veiled woman entered the pharmacy, placed a handful of guida on the counter, and asked for a bottle of carbolic acid. When Dick demurred, she lifted the veil to display an ugly flocculus growing crookedly from her chin.

"After you drink the acid, how long does it take to die?" she asked.

"Not long," Dick said. "A short wait."

Then entered Indole, who dropped his trousers, spread his great buttocks, and asked Dick to inspect him for piles.

"I see you're busy, Dick," Mrs. Moldenke said, "I'll take two ounces of the powder, a jar of mulce, and my aquafoenic, then I'll be out of your way."

IN THE WEE hours that night, a neutrodyne identified as Randall York entered Mrs. Moldenke's cabin and forced her to swallow one hundred and forty-four sewing needles after encasing them in paraffin like a mammoth pill. In a few days she complained of considerable irritation of the skin and of itching rashes. Within a week, needles were protruding from all parts of her body. Dr. Burnheart paid a call at her cabin and extracted them with pincers. In the first harvest, one hundred and forty-three were recovered from her arms, hands, breast, buttocks, feet, the lobe of the ear, the vagina, and the corner of her false eye. She said there was no pain attached to the needles' emergence, even though they came out invariably thick-end first and, unless immediately extracted, disappeared again.

Dr. Burnheart said needles inserted under the skin were known to have been borne through the muscles in many authenticated cases, coming to rest in distant parts from the place of origin, but that a needle introduced into the stomach and then emerging from the ear, as the last of Mrs. Moldenke's had, would have had to traverse the skull, which was incomprehensible.

Because he had in hand a valid waiver, no charges were filed against York, who later observed, "I got out of bed that day feeling alternately expulsive, phlegmatic, and given to hysteric depression. A crewman had found a blue, phosphorescent slime streaked the length of the ship's hull. The plesios, he said, have been active during the night. A fire began at my table today when a plate of bread combusted for no apparent reason. I ran amok."

Instead, the innocent Udo was summarily punished for the assault. An officer doused his hair with fusel oil and set it on fire. Udo ran screaming the length of the ship, then back again, until someone sloshed a bucket of seawater on him and put out the flames, at which time he fainted.

ONE STORMY EVENING the ship was struck by ball lightning, the fiery bolt entering the dining room through one of its skylights and falling to the floor in a ball of white flame. It rolled along, leaving a trail of soot and cinder in its wake, scorching shoes, cuffs, and hems before passing through a wall by burning a hole, melting the heads of nails and jarring planks from their places.

Making its way aft, charring the deck as it went, the flaming ball rolled into Moldenke's stateroom through a door carelessly, but fortunately, left ajar. Once inside, it came to rest under the bed, where its radiant heat first warmed the bedsprings, then the mattress, then Moldenke, who felt a tingling in his bones. The ball then vanished, leaving behind only a few charred splinters and a half-molten nail.

Radio Ratt:
A prodigious, five-pound death egg laid by a Russian neut, Sergei Machnov, will be exhibited for one hour only at the Katland Ice Palace following tomorrow's spankings. . . . And now, a reminder from the Ratt Administration: Necronauts cannot produce their own food and so rely for energy on existing organic matter. Settlers have reported hearing Stinkers in

DAVID OHLE

the yard, rooting in the garbage pails. "I couldn't abide them crunching bones and drinking swill all night," complained one. The President promises action soon to curb the activity. . . . Reports have arrived that the charred remains of three American tramps were found in the rubble of a charnel house fire in New Oleo today. The unidentified tramps were asleep in the cellar of the building when the fire erupted in an upstairs wastebasket full of rags.

DR. BURNHEART INVITED Ophelia for a tour of the ship's mulcing facility. With her sketchbook and charcoal sticks in hand, she followed the doctor past the incubator, with a peek into the autoclave room, then up a steep stairway to the pen where mulcing neuts were kept. Also in residence were twenty or more of the ship's cats, stationed near the pen, some inside it, all purring contentedly. A fusel lamp burning in a corner cast stark shadows against the wall.

"We've got nine of them," Dr. Burnheart said, "named after the Muses. Calliope, Terpsichore, Clio, Melpomene, Urania, et cetera. With daily draining of the dugs, they supply mulce for the whole ship." He demonstrated the procedures for feeding and watering the little group, how to examine the droppings for worms, and how to recognize dugs that were ready to be mulced. "Wait too long," he said, "and they'll burst. The membrane that covers them is paper-thin."

There were signs, Ophelia detected, of negligence: fecal material accumulating in the pen, algae in the water tubs. Several of the neuts had rotting teeth and furrowed dugs. "Dr. Burnheart, I encourage you to take more kindly to these things. They may be insensate, but we shouldn't think of them as insensitive." She began sketching a set of unhealthy dugs.

"I beg to differ," said Dr. Burnheart. "I assure you, in all my handling of them, I've never seen a sign of it. They seem absolutely dead. Animated, yes, but dead. They speak, but do not mean. It's all in the *Manifesto*. You must have read it, a woman of your education."

"Many times. Backward and forward. Edible copies and throwaways."

"Then how can you possibly take the position you do? Watch this." Stepping into the pen, he chose one of the females at random and tugged violently at her knotty queue of rich, red hair. The neut had no visible reaction, even though her vertebrae groaned audibly as her head was thrust backward.

"You see? Nothing."

"I beg to differ with *you*, Dr. Burnheart. It's right there in the *Manifesto*. Stoical endurance, yes, that they have. But not anesthesia. They suffer in some private way we can't imagine. I don't think you understand their complexity even as much as Ratt does. They have their customs, their history, whatever they can remember of it. They don't write, but they've got an oral tradition."

"Ask yourself this, what would we do without mulce?"

"I'm going to the first mate with a complaint. These pens are unsanitary in the extreme. That constitutes maltreatment of neuts, which I do think is against the law."

"Go ahead. See where that will get you."

Ophelia picked up the lamp and moved it closer to the pen. "Who is that? Someone is back there, in the dark."

"Oh, really. Where?"

She raised the lamp even higher, exposing a tableau that sickened her. The first mate, red-faced and breathing hard, dismounted one of the neuts and quickly zipped up his jumpsuit.

"You shouldn't simply barge in like this," the mate said. "Passengers are not at liberty to wander the inner sanctums of the ship as they please. And this is not at all what you might think, but rather a matter of science, industry, and experimentation. Tell her, Doctor."

"You see, Ophelia, if we service them daily, the quality of the mulce is greatly improved. All the men aboard ship have been pitching in and doing their share."

"These practices are being encouraged by the Ratt administration," the mate said. "More than encouraged. It's the law."

Burnheart said, "It triples the output and enhances the taste." He selected one of the neuts, bent his knee in genuflection, and took her dug into his mouth. She groaned pleasurably as the sucking went on and shed a tear or two when he stopped. What spilled from the doctor's full cheeks was licked up by the flock of cats.

"There you are, Ophelia. That's how it's done. Kneel down. Have a taste."

The neutrodyne rubbed her dug with mummy oil and Ophelia knelt to have a suck. Though the nipple was uncomfortably spiked with small hairs, the mulce had such a rich, sweet taste that she had trouble letting go when her mouth was full.

"You see," Dr. Burnheart said. "The quality of the mulce is directly proportional to the frequency of service. I serviced this one myself, not an hour ago. You may be shocked, you may think it bestial, but imagine the good that comes from it. And these gals don't mind. They feel nothing."

"And it restores the balance," offered the mate.

"It's right there in the *Manifesto*," Burnheart scolded. "What's bad for one may be good for all."

"The taste *is* heavenly," Ophelia said, lowering the lamp's flame.

Radio Ratt:

The heavy breathing of neutrodynes under anesthetic resounded through the narrow lanes of New Oleo on Monday when the band shell was transformed into an impromptu dental office. Three chairs were installed and more than one hundred neutrodyne teeth were extracted in the afternoon. With teeth averaging a hundred and a half guida per kilo, such exercises will be scheduled with increasing frequency for the foreseeable future. The spillage of so much blood, and the fact that it was allowed to remain wherever it fell, and there to gradually congeal, caused a great deal of slippage and loose footing among the busy dentists. Quite a few, some say, took nasty and sometimes injurious falls. . . . In Bum Bay today, neutrodyne mating season commenced. The males were spewing all over town. The sticky, threadlike material drifted in the air overhead, causing general consternation among female settlers of childbearing age. To a one, they could be seen dashing for shelter or opening parasols. The spew ranged from droplets to ten-foot globules. It was cloyingly sweet to sniff, tasty, and edible, like cotton candy.

AS THE *TITANIC* neared its anchorage off Bum Bay, passengers crowded into Der Kroetenkusser to celebrate the last hours of the voyage. The odor of the City and the sweet scent of neut spew drifted on the night wind. The Chatterjee's, a neutrodyne French horn trio, played, dancers danced, singers sang, and the sea spray felt cool and satisfying on the face.

"Yellow moon tonight," Hilter said. "Now the plagues of summer begin. I'll be glad when my feet are on solid ground at least."

Ophelia noted Mrs. Moldenke's absence.

"Mother is very sick with hemorrhagic fever," Moldenke explained. "Three nights of delirium. Red as a beet. Bleeding from half her orifices. And all this on top of her plantar wart, for which she's tried electrocautery, acids, and an ointment made of white mud, sucker weed sap, mugwort, and ground daisies, all without effect."

"The poor woman," Ophelia said. "No one has ever suffered more."

"She finds transcendence in it."

Hilter ordered a mulce. "That neut is on the way. The inventor's son. The one who loves to jabber."

"Vink," Ophelia said. "Hugo Vink."

Vink greeted them royally. "Good evening, Americans. One and all." A syrupy goo dripped from an eruption on the underside of his flocculus. *"Pardon!* Forgive me. I didn't mean to dribble. Too much root syrup on my johnnycakes. May I join you?"

"Don't be silly," Moldenke said. "Look at the size of this table. We couldn't seat the ace of spades sideways."

"No extra chairs, either," Hilter added. "Find your own table. We don't care whose son you are."

"I don't mind standing. No, sir. I could stand here seven days and seven nights and never get enough of you people and your American charm."

"In the great barnyard of intellect, neutrodyne thought is about as useful as teats on a boar hog," Hilter said.

"Say . . . have I told you people about my father's efforts at making a mirror that improves the looks of the beholder?"

"Please, go amuse yourself elsewhere," Moldenke said. "It would be such a favor to us."

"Wait, listen. My father spent many years working on the mirror, way back in the fifties. He treated glass with every chemical he could find, with dyes and solvents, curving it, running electricity through it, putting strong magnets on it, trying to get it to improve the image it reflected."

"That's a bright idea," Ophelia said. "Why couldn't you get faces to look thinner, eyes brighter, skin tone better? A mirror that flatters. A flattering mirror."

"There are plenty of empty tables over there, sir," Hilter pointed.

"Sorry. Just a tad more to go. When Father finally abandoned his attempt to make the perfect mirror, he worked tirelessly on an aerosol device that would blow donut-shaped bubbles. You'd just press the cap and thousands of donut-shaped bubbles would pour out, he thought. It was years before he discovered what any student of physics could have told him, that bubbles strive for roundness. Nature will not tolerate a donut-shaped bubble. Disheartened to be sure, he was compelled to take a turn for the dark side and move toward the development of a workable aerosol deformant."

Moldenke blew a perfect smoke ring. "Are my ears bleeding from this patter yet, Ophelia?"

Vink's flocculus throbbed, then engorged.

"He's showing his gland to us," Ophelia said excitedly.

Within the flocculus, the green gland passed from top to bottom, paused there a beat or two, then extended its tip through the flocculus opening. Vink grasped the gland with the long fingers of his three-digit hand, pulling it out to its full extent. "Have a bite, folks. I won't feel a thing. Not a nerve in my body. Completely insensate."

"Look how green it is," Ophelia said.

Moldenke salivated. "What do you think, Ophelia? Want a taste?"

She gave him a coy, reptilian look. "Oh, well, I do have an eensy weensy tiny little bit of an appetite."

"This could get you in deep trouble," said Udo. "Brand-new ordinance—no more green gland eating in public. The punishment is a greasewood burr up the rectum. Imagine the horror of extracting it. I'm telling you. You bend over, you part your buttocks, and the officer pushes it in, *backward*, with his billy club. You bleed, you fester, you cramp, you fever. Some die."

"They say the taste of fresh gland is otherworldly," said Ophelia.

"Here, have a bite. Please." Vink lowered his head, making the gland more accessible.

Ophelia bit off a small piece for tasting. "Mmmmmmmm. Oh, Moldenke. You must try it. You must!" She took a second, larger bite and a green froth formed at the corner of her mouth.

Moldenke bent over and had a bite, followed by Hilter. By then, the gland was severely reduced.

"Don't worry," Vink said. "It'll grow back by morning."

Radio Ratt:
Bauble Porch, a Pisstown neut, was watching the spankings last Sunday when, forgetful of her balance, she jumped up in her excitement, stepped forward, and fell fifty feet to the rock-hard, blood-spattered ice below. Because neutrodynes believe that such sudden, premature, or accidental deaths are not entirely final, efforts at preserving the body are often made. In the Porch case, the restoration was carried out at Dr. Ferry's New Oleo facility. She was placed on a firm, cypress board and her clothing removed. The bones of the nose were cracked with

a chisel and mallet, then a hooked wire was inserted to draw cerebral matter through the nostrils and into the mouth. When the mouth was full, the lips were sewn shut and the remaining cerebral matter discarded. Prior to cleansing the cavity with astringent soap, an incision was made and all contents of the abdomen except the kidneys and several hydatid cysts were removed. The diaphragm was then cut to allow access to the pulmonary implants, thought to be in top condition and reusable. Finally, Porch was packed with greasewood shavings, cosmetics were applied, and she was taken to the Neutrodyne Hall rotunda, where she will remain on exhibit until the tenth of Fog.

AS THE *TITANIC* underwent docking maneuvers in Bum Bay harbor, Del Piombo offered to buy Moldenke a double mulce.

"Moldenke," Piombo said. "We think we can use someone like you. All voyage long we've had an ear to your private conversations. We've closeted ourselves in your cabin and kept an eye on you in your private moments."

"We?"

"Yes, We. Myself and my partner, taking turns. My partner will remain anonymous in all this."

"All this?"

"Don't you read the papers? The new laughing laws. Ratt is out of control. We no longer stand for it. Let them catch you wearing a frown and you could go to your death. They've stopped printing waivers, raising the value of existing ones tenfold. And let's not talk about the thriving market in fakes and forgeries."

"I've been trying to get one."

"We'll provide you with as many as you need to get out of trouble."

"Trouble?"

"We'll do everything we can to make sure you get through this alive and free."

"Through what?"

"We're going to take action against Ratt. If we succeed, chaos will follow . . . for an indeterminate period. It may trigger another Forgetting. The territory isn't charted. Are you with us?"

"Who are you? I mean, the us. Who's the us?"

"Us . . . my partner and I. There are others, thousands, but we'll be doing the dirty work. You and us."

"The three of us."

"Yes."

"And the work? The dirty work?"

"Here is a wog of guida. Check in at the old Adolphus Hotel. It's walking distance to Dilly Plaza. Take a small room. Our seed money is limited."

"I could stay with Mother at her Bum Bay mansion."

"No, no. She's too much in the news. Stay at the Adolphus and go about your ordinary business. Blend in. Establish regular daily habits. Listen to the radio. Be seen. Go places and be seen. Get a bank account. Look for a job. We'll be in touch."

Piombo clicked the heels of his clogs, shook Moldenke's hand, and before joining other disembarking passengers on the gang plank said, "And by all means, get a haircut."

"Yes, a haircut. I will." Moldenke transferred the soggy guida from one hand to another, feeling its weight. His life was dull enough, he thought, despite the small terrors that littered it. Why not start trying to keep things in balance, he wondered, and seek excitement? Assuming his hearts could stand the strain.

Radio Ratt:

Now, a message from the President: "Because I remain committed to easing tensions between Stinker and settler populations, I beg you, my good people, please, remember, what carrion is to vultures, fungu *is to Stinkers. So don't let the bulbs get a toehold anywhere in or around your living quarters. If you see them, wherever they are, drench them with vinegar or touch a candle flame to them until they burn away. Deny Stinkers what they most hunger for and they won't be lurking on your property. Good night and good luck to you all."*

WHILE HIS MOTHER returned to her Bum Bay mansion, Moldenke took a sooty-ceilinged, three-walled room at the old Adolphus. Furnished only with a pull-down bed, a wicker chair, a table, a radio, and a fusel-oil lamp that sputtered and smoked, it was not only all the accommodation he needed, it was all he was entitled to by his agreement with Piombo.

After a dreamless night of deep sleep, Moldenke awoke at dawn to find a neutrodyne sergeant sitting at the foot of his bed, browsing in Sunday's *Observer*, and drinking soured mulce.

"I'm here to arrest you, Moldenke. Get up and get dressed."

Moldenke's hearts constricted. Two of them nearly stopped. "The charge?"

"Murdering the captain of the *Titanic* . . . and eating uncooked green gland in a public place. Confess, please, and we can get on with the punishment. Unless, of course, you have a valid waiver."

"Where do you get one? I've tried every way I know."

"That information is privileged. If you have no waiver, it's time to face these charges."

"I'm innocent, of course, waiver or no. Everyone knows it was the cabin boy."

"Perhaps. But, as Ratt sees it, the innocent suffer along with the guilty. It's the law. Collective guilt, collective punishment. Unless . . ."

"Unless you have a waiver. But they've already hung a neut for this."

"You don't mean to besmirch the Court's reputation for fairness and efficiency, do you?"

"Not at all."

"That kind of attitude could land you in the French Sewer for life, or get you hung."

"I did not kill the captain of the *Titanic*. A mountain of evidence can attest to that. There are witnesses, alibis—"

"That's all well and good, but let me explain the situation in detail to you, so that things will run smoothly and efficiently and this mess will be brought to a satisfactory conclusion without a great deal of pissing and moaning. Now then, according to current law, killing the captain of a sea liner is not deemed a felony. Moving your bowels on a carpet, however, is more than just a trifle. You tack that onto the charge, and you'll likely get a good long stay in the Sewer . . . at the very least."

"I'm going to plead not guilty."

"That's a judicial nuisance. You'd only be heavily fined. Frankly, I don't understand your take on this. Whosoever killed the captain will eventually pay the price. No one eludes the sweep of Ratt's law for long. It's the most elegant system ever devised. Someday, perhaps, you'll watch an innocent party hang for something you've done. Really, there's no better feeling than that. The time will come, the time will come. You people will eventually see things the way Ratt sees them."

PRESIDENT RATT FLEW his new Vink-designed orbigator from Indiana to Bum Bay. Upon landing the craft, he came out of the pilothouse dressed in a fleece bathing suit and a rubber cap. Then, stepping through a curtain of steam that hissed from the ship's engines, he said, "A glorious machine. It raises me up like a loaf and sets me down like a stone."

It being President Kenny Day, he offered his prayers to Arvey for all those condemned to labor on days of rest and refreshment, for drivers serving on the pedal buses, for servants, bellhops, and small boys on golf courses.

He and his Arvian attendants then set out by pedal cab for Noah's, a floating restaurant. As soon as Ratt was safely aboard, the restaurant left the dock amid a cloud of cooking odors, the waiters taking orders and serving drinks.

Ophelia Balls, dining alone, seemed the obvious choice as Ratt's dinner companion. He dismissed his attendants and came to her table, using a nicely carved greasewood cane, more an affectation than a necessity it appeared. Its tip made contact with the deck only every third or fourth step. In the interim it swung like a pendulum from his stiffened forefinger. Without asking, he sat with her, wiping his shapeless mustache with the back of his hand. "The mud duck is very good here," he said. "Freshly killed."

The waiter came. Ophelia ordered the mud duck in brown sauce and a glass of fermented mulce. Without looking at the menu, Ratt ordered raw death eggs and a glass of plain mulce.

"You may be interested in knowing," Ratt said, "that before assuming the presidency, I employed 175 neutrodynes in my Pisstown hair mill. It used to be I couldn't stand the things. When my late father brought home the first one, Rags, I didn't even want to be around it. I wanted to keep it away from me in another room, or out in the toolshed. I changed my mind after reading a poem by Baxter Sincay, the settler poet, which concluded with the line, 'Only a neut would spend its last breath in a kiss for its murderer's hand.'

"After Rags, came Ned, then Alfred, Limpy, Roy, Hank, Andrew, Wulfe, Ack Ack, Stagger, and more than 150 others of all sizes, lineage, and description. Most were strays who found their way to my father's butcher shop looking for scraps. Others were dropped off by owners who tired of them. Those poor things didn't have anyone to look after them but me, I thought, and I vowed that as long as I lived, the neuts would never want for anything."

Ratt whisked a sawfly from the tabletop. Ophelia took advantage of the pause to say, "I've read your *Manifesto*, sir. You married a neut it said."

"Back in '06, when I went to the Tektite desert and trained to pull pedal buses with my teeth and a rope. There I met Sabetha, pretty, tender, tiny, toothless. My first love. In a fever, we wed. Three babies were born. One had spina bifida, one was still, one was swiped by a band of kidnappers and sold to a deformist surgeon. Out of grief, I elected to put my own belly on the line for neutrodyne charities. I pulled pedal train cars until my ribs broke. I let ponies kick me hard in the tush. People slammed my breadbasket with brickbats. Gradually, my midsection toughened."

"Fascinating stuff. Tell me more."

"I'm a fan of Khalil Gibran. Surely you noticed his influence on the *Manifesto*. He was known as the Prophet of Lebanon in the Age of Sinatra, you know. I've committed most of his work to memory."

Aside from Ratt's general rudeness, Ophelia was put off by his affected mannerisms, incessant brushing of imaginary crumbs from the table, blowing his nose with great ceremony, and obsessively folding and refolding his handkerchief.

"Gibran wrote a very good piece on death," he went on. "He goes off to a field to meditate, to get away from the crowd. In the corner of the field, under some trees, is a small graveyard. Inspired by this, he sets out to compare the city of the living and the city of the dead, dwelling on the eternal silence of death and the endless sorrow of life. Then a funeral procession comes along. A rich man is being buried—musicians, incense, all the trappings. Gibran takes note of this and watches the careful and luxurious ceremonies that take place—all befitting a man of influence and stature—someone of value. . . ."

The mulces were brought. Ratt pointed his knife at Ophelia's glass. "If people only knew what fermentation does to their eee-so-faygus, they wouldn't touch it." Then he pressed on and spoke even louder about Gibran: "So, later, another funeral comes by. This time it's a poor man. His shabby family trails along, the wife with an infant, the mangy dog, the hungry children. What do they do? They just throw the wooden casket into a ditch."

The eggs and the duck came. Ratt dug in hungrily, continuing to speak with his cavernous mouth full of dark yolk. "This inspired Gibran and he waxed eloquent: 'I looked at the city of the living and said to myself, "That place belongs to the few." Then I looked upon the trim city of the dead and said, "That place, too, belongs to the few. Oh, Lord, where is the haven of all people?" And as he said this, he looked up at the sky and the clouds and the sun's long and beautiful, golden rays, and he heard a voice within him saying, "Over there!"'" With a thin, white finger Ratt pointed in the direction of the ogling Indiana sun. "Over there!"

"Over where, exactly?" Ophelia asked. "I don't understand."

"Well, you can't be too analytical when it comes to mystics. I simply let the man's thoughts rumble like thunder o'er the prairie of my mind." Ratt chuckled mysteriously, a low, wolfish growl. "I'll tell you this, though . . . whatever your name is . . ."

"Ophelia Balls. American. Bum Bay City."

"I'll tell you this, Ophelia . . . here we only come to meet. We are only passersby. One day our memories, like dry leaves, will blow away in a Great Forgetting. Meanwhile, let us live in peace and war, with pain and pleasure in equal measure. Come, rejoice. Every Forgetting is a renewal, not a loss. We have life after life after life. Like an annual flower, like the Edelweiss, brand new every spring. And another thing to tuck under your Vink, Ophelia . . . man is a laughing animal. There are lower animals that laugh. The crow, the goose, the hyena, the owl, and the jackass all laugh in their own way. Many men laugh like geese. Some have the canine laugh. This has given me the idea for a Laughter in the Streets program. I want to hear outrageous cackling everywhere I go. That's on my agenda. Obligatory laughing. We see you wearing a frown . . . we catch you shedding a tear . . . you'll pay with a long stay in the Sewer. . . or maybe a big burr right up the kazoo."

Ophelia laughed nervously. "Very sound thinking, sir. But may I ask something?"

"Of course you may."

"It concerns waivers . . . how to get them . . . and where to get them. Mine is . . . used up. I have a friend who's looking for one, too."

There was a loud bump, a splash, and a collective gasp from the diners. Someone shouted, "Neut overboard!"

To Ophelia's great surprise, it was Ratt who was the first to plunge through the tangle of water hyacinth into the murky water, followed by a half-dozen Arvian attendants.

Most diners stood at the rail and watched the rescue efforts. Some continued eating in silence. In about an hour, with no trace other than a soggy cap, the search for the neut was abandoned and *Noah's* returned to the dock.

Ratt crossed paths with Ophelia as she walked to her pedal car. Wet and muddy, he had a rotted, swampy odor. "I tell you, that poor neut is down in the silt by now. There was blood on the cap."

"Too bad. Too bad. Sir?"

"What is it? I'm in something of a rush. Mercy Council meeting at onety-two and a half."

"Waivers. I was asking you how to get one."

"Oh, very easy, very easy. As a matter of fact, that's topic number one at today's meeting."

"Good, then . . . where do I—?"

"Look at the time. I'm already late." Shivering, he got into his cab and closed the door. When it pedaled away, a group of diners held out their hands to congratulate Ophelia on her brush with greatness.

"Something to treasure for a lifetime," one said.

AFTER AN EXHAUSTING crosstown pedal bus ride, Moldenke appeared in the petty claims court at the Rattery before the neutrodyne magistrate, Irma Noodle.

"Ma'am," said the arresting officer, "his name is Moldenke, up for the murder of that ship captain, and eating uncooked green gland . . . in public."

The magistrate banged her gavel. "Does he have a waiver, Sergeant?"

"No waiver, Miss Noodle."

"I *am* innocent, though," Moldenke said.

"We'll have none of that kind of talk in my court room, mister," the magistrate said.

"I warned him," the sergeant said, jabbing his billy club into Moldenke's ribs.

The magistrate glared at Moldenke viciously. "Step forward, you. What a disgrace you are. Remember this, humiliation is that sweet root from which all virtues shoot. I hereby sentence you to an indeterminate length of public humiliation, to be served in the French Sewer beginning at sunup tomorrow. Will the arresting sergeant please see to it this offender is on hand there for the morning rush . . . to get him started on the right foot."

"It will be my pleasure, Miss Noodle."

"Take him off, then. Next case."

Another sergeant stepped to the bench with a red-haired settler boy, his prisoner.

Moldenke's sergeant said, "There goes an interesting case. Young settler, nine years old, sells unripe green gland to a blind man. Noodle is pitiless with these young grifters. I can almost guarantee the lad'll get something prickly up his bung. And if she's in a bad mood, they'll coat it in phosphate first."

With firm assurances that he would report to the Sewer as directed, Moldenke was allowed to spend the night in his room.

"Do be there," the sergeant said, with a chuckle. "If you're not, I'll come after you. And when I catch you, I'll unscrew that navel and let your legs fall off."

THAT EVENING MOLDENKE'S eye was attracted to an ad in the Entertainment & Diversions section of the *Observer*.

Tonite
At the Bum Bay Ice Palace
Purgeth and St. Dizier
French Spanking Team

Why not? he thought. *My last night a free man.*

Taking along a heavy neut-hair sweater, he caught a pedal bus to the Ice Palace. Promptly at eight, a sergeant skated to the center of the ring and the show was underway: "Ladies and gents . . . welcome to the spankings. We've got an exciting agenda tonight, so sit back and behold the very best . . . that great French spanking duo—Purgeth and St. Dizier."

A round of applause greeted the artful duo as they appeared on the ice. An offender was brought in wearing a black sackcloth jacket and breakaway trousers. Purgeth and St. Dizier skated in narrowing circles around the short, plump American, the blades of their skates cutting deeply into the ice and sending cool showers of it everywhere.

The sergeant announced, "For unlawful congress with Stinkers . . . three good whacks." Purgeth had the paddles in a sack slung over his shoulders and St. Dizier pulled a cart supplied with absorbent towels and strong liniment.

"All right," said the sergeant. "The spankings will begin. Who'll come down and be the first?"

From the shadows on the far side of the Ice Palace, Ophelia, Vinkless, walked onto the ice. Moldenke's hearts fluttered. He rose on tiptoe to see over the big neut in front of him. Everyone in the crowded arena stood, eager for the first spanking of the evening. The neut kindly offered to let Moldenke sit on his shoulders. Moldenke declined instinctively, thought better of it, and accepted the invitation. Now he had an unobstructed view. He peeled a half-zil from his roll and stuffed it into the neut's pocket.

"Thank you, sir. You want some green gland?"

"No, no, thank you."

"I got waivers," the neut said, showing Moldenke a handful. "Take one. My compliments. And don't forget to vote Ratt."

Moldenke had not felt such elation at chancing on something precious since walking over a sewer grate and spotting an antique silver quarter. He folded the waiver with care and precision. "Ratt it is then. I was undecided."

"That's the spirit," the neut said. "When you're Ratt, you can't be wrong."

"All right. We have a woman with spirit," the sergeant shouted. "Prisoner, take your position." The prisoner aligned his skates with a red stripe on the ice, then bent forward. The officer tugged at the breakaway trousers until the rump section pulled away, exposing a wide, callused bottom.

"All right. We have position and we have a target."

Purgeth opened the sack of wooden paddles and Ophelia chose one with a shaft made of greasewood and inset with small metal spikes. She then approached the spanking line and readied herself. Her first swing was off the mark, a glancing blow that bounced the paddle up the prisoner's spine and against the head.

"All right, lady. Have another go. Aim for the moon."

Ophelia's swat landed squarely and the prisoner moved forward on his skates. The sergeant took the measurement. "A hair less than a gibnut's tail . . . try again."

St. Dizier splashed liniment on the prisoner's rump and wiped away some of the new blood. "Try again, dear."

Ophelia swung with such force the second time, the slap of the paddle echoed through all the reaches of the Ice Palace and propelled the American forward at least a tail and a half.

"A fine showing, kiddo. Next? Next one up?"

St. Dizier applied more liniment to the bleedings and went to work with a fresh towel. Ophelia retired to the shadows. Moldenke lost sight of her even from his high vantage.

"What's your name, neut?" he asked.

"Georgie Boy."

"Georgie . . . I wonder . . . as long as I'm up here, would you walk me to the other side? There's someone over there I want to find." He stuffed another note into the neut's pocket.

The neut made his way to the other side, trotting when a break in the crowd allowed it. His uneven gait jostled Moldenke, who twice fell backward and would have crashed to the floor if the neut hadn't caught him. The search for Ophelia continued unsuccessfully until the spankings were over and the neut was swept off his feet by the exiting throng. In falling, he contrived to land on his back, providing Moldenke a soft landing and preventing any injury.

Radio Ratt:

It is not in anyone's best interest to breed for intelligence in neutrodynes. Just as we need an educated class of settlers to run the mills and distribute the guida, we surely need an ignorant army of neutrodyne workers and consumers. How else can the delicate machinery of demand be maintained? Neutrodynes

*should be advised at every opportunity that they are a miser-
able, loutish bunch and must always beg for improvement and
change. We shall divide them into hostile groups by constantly
harping on pseudocontroversy and matters of slight importance.
Moreover, we will destroy their faith in natural leaders and
favored political candidates by holding them up to ridicule,
contempt, and scorn.*

AT SIX A.M. the following morning, Moldenke stood outside
the entrance to the French Sewer, waiting for the arrival of
the Superintendent, along with twoty or threety other
waiverless miscreants.

"Look sharp, now," said the sergeant in charge. "Don't be
dawdling or spitting. When the Superintendent arrives, his
wagon will be bringing your clean white tunics, your rubber
boots, your blue berets, and a good supply of *rabots* . . . the
long poles you'll be using to break up blockages and prod the
material along. Are there any questions? Yes . . . you. The
lady in the rear. State your name, please, and origin."

It was a voice Moldenke knew well. "Ophelia Balls, out of
Pisstown." She held up her sketch pad. "I'd like to ask . . .
am I permitted to make sketches inside?"

"I don't see the harm there, as long as you perform your
duties."

Moldenke raised his hand. "Sir. Moldenke, out of
Indiana."

"One name only?"

"Yessir. Lost the first one in the Great Forgetting."

"Your question then?"

"Where do we spend the night? Are there living quarters
in there?"

"Living, dining, bathing, and sleeping quarters, all inside."

"Thank you, sir."

When the Superintendent arrived, the sergeant barked, "Attention now. Listen carefully to Mr. Montfaucon while you put on your tunics and boots."

Moldenke's spirits sank further when he saw that it was the same Montfaucon he'd encountered aboard the *Titanic.* He knew now that his days here would be restless and worrisome.

Montfaucon spoke through an *Observer* rolled into a cone, his eye socket now eggless and empty. A squat, pig-headed man, his high-pitched squeal grated on Moldenke's ear. "The procedure is simple. Use the *rabot* to break up clumps when you see them. Push the material along. Let the water do its work without all that obstruction."

When Moldenke leaned against a banquette to pull on his boots, Ophelia was doing the same on the other side. "Ophelia, what are you here for?"

"For vomiting up a bucketful of horsehead pudding in Dilly Plaza last night after the spankings. They confiscated my thinker. Too much celebrating, I suppose. And I was out of waivers. Used my last one when they accused me of dallying with a neut. He was the sweetest thing. Had a little kiosk on North Street, right next to the Squat 'n' Gobble. Sold roasted grasshoppers, contraband hair, edible books, that sort of stuff. I absolutely must get another waiver. I understand Ratt's Mercy Council issues them."

"I got one from a neut, at the spankings."

"Did you, now? I wouldn't put any faith in it. Most of them are bogus. A little prank neuts like to play."

Moldenke looked at his waiver. It was blank.

"Vink Ink," Ophelia explained. "They put blue dye in an alkaline solution. When this 'ink' is applied, it absorbs carbon dioxide from the air and forms an acid, which changes the dye to colorless."

"Marvelous, just marvelous. Where does it meet, the Council? Where are its offices?"

"Neutrodyne Hall, no doubt."

"The moment I get out of here, that's where I'll head. It's up on Arden Boulevard, isn't it?"

"I don't know. I thought it was out past the orbigator field."

Moldenke tugged at the arm of another prisoner. "Say, friend. Any idea where I might find Neutrodyne Hall?"

"It burned to the ground yesterday. Chewing gum factory across the street exploded. Sent flaming chicle through the second-story windows, igniting the carpets."

"Bad news. Bad news. Oh, well, would you happen to know where I might get one of those waivers . . . the ones that exempt you from—"

"You can't get them anymore. They're plumb out. Friend told me they was planning on printing some more, but, hell, I don't know, he's pretty much of a liar."

"This is absurd and unreasonable!" Moldenke grumbled under his breath, stamping his foot on the wet, slime-coated stone. His shoulders sank under the weight of his predicament. "This is an outrage to reason. Sharing the guilt, sharing the punishment. Ridiculous!"

Montfaucon peeked through a rust hole in the entrance door, then turned to address the prisoners, swaying right to left, then forward and backward, on the balls of his feet. "Today, being a Monday, and yesterday, being President Kenny Day, I wouldn't be surprised to see very, very heavy clumping. And we must be quick. Remember, the tour boats begin running very shortly. Take your positions along either wall and have your *rabots* at the ready."

The sergeant called out, "It's just about opening time. And for Pete's sake, take a few deep breaths while you can."

The tall iron doors of the Sewer entrance yawned open, freeing a burst of warm, foul-smelling air.

Montfaucon made his final statements. "Do not forget. This Sewer is a spectacle of enlightenment, so well-maintained that a lady dressed in her finest can take a boat tour from the President's Home to the Ice Palace without fear of fatigue and without stepping in anything unclean."

As the prisoners marched slowly into the Sewer, a shower of condensation rained on them from the arched stone ceiling. By the time they had begun to move the clumps along, their tunics were soaking wet.

The first tour boat of the day came round a bend in the trench. Well-dressed Germans, men and women, sat in comfortable seats. Two of the men were firing small-caliber pistols at gibnuts hiding in nooks and crannies of the stonework.

The tour guide offered commentary: "Everyone knows that no foreigner of distinction wants to leave Bum Bay's Frenchtown without making this singular trip. Notice the rows of lamps, each provided with its silvered reflector. See how they light up the vaulted gallery and cast their reflections in the black, turgid water at our feet. Don't the white-robed prisoners look like so many ghosts? People who have seen everything say the French Sewer Complex is perhaps the most beautiful sight in the world. The temperature is so mild, the odor so slight that—"

A fusillade of gunshots rang out. Moldenke's knees lost all sensation and he sank to the ground, groaning. Had it not been for Ophelia's thrusting out her *rabot* to stop him, he would have rolled into the trench. "I'm hit!" He spit blood. Ophelia examined his mouth and found that the bullet had entered one cheek, smashed his only sound tooth, and lay like a leaden pill on his tongue.

"Not serious," she said. "Don't make a commotion. Don't get Montfaucon excited."

Moldenke spat out the flattened disk of lead and the crumbs of his tooth.

"Here comes Montfaucon," a prisoner hissed. "He's got a terrible temper."

Montfaucon was pulling a German tourist along by the collar. "Goddamned kraut! You won't be shooting any more prisoners while I'm around."

"Too late," Ophelia said.

Montfaucon stood the German in front of Moldenke. "You've put a hole in this man's face. What do you have to say for yourself?"

The German shrugged. "An accident, *Monsieur*. I was aiming at a gibnut."

As the German's *eau de parfum* sweetened the heavy air, Moldenke passed his little finger through the hole in his cheek. Ophelia fixed the scene in her mind. Later, free of the sewer, she would sketch it.

"Typical Teutonic response. Now, you see that clump there, in the ditch? Do you?"

"*Ja, ja.*"

"Get down on your knees and have a mouthful of it!"

"*Acht!*"

"You *vaaaant* me to shoot you?" Montfaucon placed the barrel of the pistol in the German's ear. "With such a small projectile, intended for a soft-bodied gibnut, you could be left addle-brained the rest of your misbegotten life. Better to eat some *Scheiß*, I'd say." The hammer of the pistol cocked with a snap that echoed up and down the lamplit tunnel.

The German submitted to the humiliation, kneeling and keeping his head close to the floor until he had swallowed the mouthful. He could be heard to weep, in bursts, throughout the process, and when it was all over, he knelt beside the ditch and threw it all back up.

Montfaucon gave the pistol to Moldenke. "Here, shoot him. Tit for tat."

Though his jaw and mouth were ablaze with pain, Moldenke had no urge to shoot the man. "If it was an accident . . . I'd just as soon let him go. He's had enough, I think."

"All right, then. He says to let you go." Montfaucon placed the pistol again in the German's ear, this time firing two shots in quick succession. Unconscious, perhaps dead, the German fell into the trench. "There, you're free to go. . . . All right, prisoners. Now you've got a true clump of shit to push with your *rabots*. Get busy. Except you." He was pointing at Ophelia. "You'll come along with me. An officer awaits to take you into custody. A very serious charge."

"The charge?" Ophelia asked.

"Why, killing an innocent German by shooting him twice in the head. Isn't it perfectly obvious?"

Montfaucon hurled Ophelia's sketch pad into the trench and escorted her out of the Sewer into the bright noonday sun.

As the tourists moved on, Moldenke and several other prisoners took up their *rabots* and gave the German a firm push, freeing the body to be drawn along briskly in the wake of the boat.

Radio Ratt:
An American sponge-dryer living on Square Island was gathering barrel sponges when he saw a hut near a lamasery. Inside, on cots, he found a male and a female Stinker with a

DAVID OHLE

*child. The male was asleep on one cot. The female was feeding
the child white melon on the other. The American went away,
but revisited the hut on three successive nights. Each time he
found the male asleep and the female, bare-breasted and wearing a platinum amulet, feeding melon to the child. At last, on
the fifth day, he arrived to find the female and child asleep. He
chloroformed the mother and struck her in the head with a
wooden mallet until she was dead. The child he drowned in the
slop bucket. The male he let live. On President Kenny Day, the
American will be awarded the Ratt Cross for valor.*

EXCLUSIVE TO THE *Observer*.

The Michael Ratt Interview

G.H. My first thought is, thank you so much for finding
the time to talk to the *Observer*.

M.R. I've always said that since the modern period ended
with the last Forgetting, we've needed a new form of jour-
nalism. Ordinary news, that turgid, repetitive, sludge of
minutiae, no longer meets the needs of a myth-starved pop-
ulace. That's why I admire the *Observer* as I do. Your news
is very, very extraordinary. Also, I agree with Chesterton,
that the press of old was merely a machine for destroying
the public memory, existing solely to wash away the popular recollection of yesterday.

G.H. Spare time must be a rare commodity for you.
When you have some, how do you spend it?

M.R. I make pretzels. How I love them. And when they
are taken from the oven, they have a wonderful shine. This
comes from dipping them in a weak, harmless solution of
caustic soda. I love to sail, too, and to fish for plesios from
my yacht, the *Pipistrelle*. I cure them in borax. It takes a
hundred days. The crust will turn black and you can polish

it like a shoe. After a hundred years, you could still saw it open and eat it.

G.H. What was your first act upon assuming office?

M.R. I ordered my budget committee to strike the salary of the public executioner and the cost of the stone she used to sharpen her glinty guillotine.

G.H. Word has leaked that you plan to outlaw the use of maps. Can that be true?

M.R. Maps are all wrong. Every one ever made. Sure, you say, looking at a map, "Indian Apple is a big city." But how big is a map? Not very. And yet, when we read maps, we somehow expect the place to be big, even though the map is very little.

G.H. What can you tell us of your plans for the future?

M.R. Plans are plans, not maps. What is superimposed on a map, a plan, is like a leaf on the ground, easily blown away.

G.H. You've always managed to keep your private life under wraps, away from the limelight.

M.R. With one notable exception.

G.H. Big Baby Frances?

M.R. In a hush-hush Pisstown ceremony I took a second wife after mourning Sabetha ten years, according to the neutrodyne way. But unsuitable pudenda broke that marriage apart very fast. You see, it would have required an elephantine *member virile* to scratch those great carnal itches of hers, so the sex was for the most part oral. In my mouth, what masked as her clitoris, some thick-skinned slug-like thing that looked like a two-pound bivalve, became so engorged it choked me, though she twittered with joy when I sank my pointy, sharp teeth into it. Frances and I were divorced, publicly, in 1945. She died of the flu at the age of fifty-seven. In despair, I bought a hurdy-gurdy and a trained monkey. I prospered that way for a time, but came into money when the carriage of a wealthy mill owner ran over my monkey and burst the hurdy-gurdy. The generous settlement provided the seed money for me to "throw my hat into the ring," as they used to say in Kenny's day.

G.H. We know so little of your early years, of your family.

M.R. Because of a congenital deformity, my mother stood but three feet high and weighed forty stones. That, taken with the scaly, chitinous appearance of the flesh on her back, was certain to paint the picture of a great sea tortoise in the mind's eye. She was born in Indiana's Bloomberg, a rural village. One day she was fishing and caught a terrapin. When she tried to get it off the hook she was bitten. She cursed the terrapin, all terrapins. She was pregnant with me at the time. That's why I came out looking this way.

G.H. You refer to the greenish pallor and the scaly, olive-shaped head?

M.R. Yes, and the cold blood. You see, she marked all her children in different ways. A brother was born missing a little finger because my father severed a pinkie while slaughtering a French pig. My sister was marked by a tame gibnut. Seems one frigid night Mother put johnnycakes in the oven to bake, slammed the door, and stuffed the firebox with wood, not aware that the pet gibnut had crawled into the oven to get warm. It was not until the odor of burning fur filled the house that anyone realized the animal's predicament. As a result, my sister was born with a hairy tail and very large yellow eyes. To this day she sleeps next to the stove and purrs contentedly. Even so, she leads an active life, studies Arvianism, paints, runs a chain of squats in the Fertile Crescent, and does very well for herself. In onety-one, three other sisters perished in a sailing accident. This sent me to bed with grief. The room was darkened and sealed against drafts. I remained in seclusion five years and grew violets in a window box in an attempt to recollect the countryside. Under these circumstances my lungs declined. I was delirious and near death a dozen times. No sooner had I recovered from that, two aged brothers committed suicide by eating poisoned corn. Both had suffered reverses in their attempts to curb the market, one in hair and one in neut teeth. They met in Dilly Plaza one day, then retired to the Grassy Knoll and ate the deadly corn.

G.H. The Stinker problem, sir. Can you address that publicly? And why is Stinker spelled with a capital "S"?

M.R. The "S" is to grant them the dignity they deserve. We didn't always call them Stinkers, you know. Not many readers are aware that I come from a long line of Stinkers, a lineage that began in an iron-age peat bog somewhere on Square Island. That's where they dug up my grand greatfather, Morgan Ratt. The event made news back then, before that big Forgetting in '52. He had apparently been strangled in a religious sacrifice a thousand years before that, and the sweet bog juices preserved him in such good condition, they were able to bring him back. The press of the time coined the term "necronaut" and applied it to grandpa in every headline: "Necronaut Walks! Necronaut Talks. Necronaut Miracle—A Dead Man Lives." Morgan became a rookie with Cincinnati and they elected him to the All-Star squad. That year Wally Post, the second necronaut to be brought back, electrified the bleachers with his 565-foot home run. That was then, though. Today's Stinkers are a sorry, sorry lot. There was an occasion during the Chaos that found me driving my pedal car toward the Pisstown front when I was set upon by a band of Stinkers. They didn't do anything to snuff my wick at once, and when I fainted from the awful agonies they inflicted on me, my face was drenched with stale Stinker piss to revive me so they could commence new and more ingenious tortures. When it seemed I could bear no more, the younger members of the band got about me and laughed at my apish shrieks, then fed twigs to a slow greasewood fire that burned on my belly. The next day and the day after that, I supplied fun for the Stinker encampment. A comely young female tried to make me open my mouth so that she could defecate into it. When I refused, she took a brickbat lying by and knocked my teeth in one by one, then used a rough pair of wooden pincers to grasp my tongue by its root and drag me all over the camp, convulsed with mirth over my sufferings. On the last day, I supplied entertainment and sport for the Stinker children, who staked me to a mud bank and enjoyed breaking my feet in the fashion of *bastinado* by clubbing them until every one of the bones was broken and the flesh reduced to jelly. On the third day, signs indicated the Stinkers were breaking camp. As a parting memento, they cleft my chin with a corn knife and shot me in the head, though not fatally. I'll go to my grave with an irretrievable bullet resting in my brain pan.

G.H. Yet you've inaugurated programs to bring them back in huge numbers. "A Stinker in every garage," I believe you said. "And a roasted gibnut at every table."

M.R. Exuberance, insouciance, call it what you will. Those were the heady days of my first administration, just after that crusty old crab Dorothy Teeters got ridden out of town on a flaming French pig.

G.H. Peters?

M.R. Sorry, I forgot. Where were we?

G.H. The overproduction of Stinkers.

M.R. While I'm not apologizing for the Stinker programs, which, as a whole, have been very successful, I do remember the first wave of them that washed over us. They were so hungry we left bread crusts and eggs out for them. Then they were coming in packs, squatting all over the countryside, hissing and spitting at one another with a deafening noise. They sometimes filled wooden buckets with water and sat in the round like children at a game, using their hands to catch the moon's reflection. Once we stopped leaving food out for them, they showed a talent for opening locks. They entered our kitchens, our smokehouses, and helped themselves to what was ours. We'd find the mulce jar overturned. We'd find piles of their steaming stool in the alley. Uprooted ferns in the hothouse. You name it.

G.H. Your Stinker heritage. May we go back to that?

M.R. Morgan married a settler female and the union resulted in eighty crossbreeds. Some of them followed the precedent set by Greatpa Ratt and bred with Stinkers. Others married settlers. That's the line I come from. So, I'm only part Stinker.

G.H. They say some Stinkers remember the other times, the times before the Forgettings.

M.R. That belief is certainly afoot these days. Let's end this, Gerald. It's time for my flying lesson.

G.H. One more question, sir?

M.R. Of course.

G.H. Rumors persist that there's a plot.

M.R. The plot to take my life? It's scarcely a rumor. To the plotters, I say, "Kiss my big ass purple." That's all, Gerald.

MRS. MOLDENKE, FEELING unusually fit one morning, put on her clogs and pedal pushers and pedaled her little canvas-canopied car all the way to Pisstown to attend the dedication of a newly built Arvian temple. Also in attendance was Michael Ratt's Secretary of Neutrodyne Affairs, Vincent Goop, a noted Pisstown mill owner. An honor guard of plume-hatted Arvians drew up to see Mr. Goop dedicate their new temple.

Once inside the structure, visitors had to keep moving, never looking too long at the Arvey facsimile floating in a pool of light that fell from the domed, glass roof. An Arvian choir stood near the catafalque, reciting Arvey's legendary *Last List* again and again, in hypnotically monotonous voices: "Typing . . . crystal for watch . . . job . . . bank account . . . mail . . . job . . . haircut . . . library . . . plug for radio . . . haircut . . ."

On his way to the podium, Mr. Goop stepped on something slippery and almost fell. Mrs. Moldenke, walking just behind him, acted quickly, grasping the collar of Goop's coat and breaking what could have been a nasty fall.

"There you are, Mr. Goop, no damage done."

Righting himself, Goop looked at the bottom of his clog. Stuck there were the flattened, slimy remains of a thumb-sized slug. "Good God," Goop said, looking directly at Mrs. Moldenke. "You've squashed a temple slug. These slugs are descendants of the one found in Arvey's casket."

An angry neutrodyne sergeant rushed toward her. "You're going to be cited for this! Name, please."

"Agnes Moldenke."

The sergeant took a step backward and adjusted his goggles. "*The* Agnes Moldenke. Mother of edible guida?"

"Yes. That's me. But I'm certainly not the one who stepped on the slug. It was him, Mr. Goop. There it is on his clog."

"Who stepped on the slug, Mr. Goop?" the sergeant asked.

"That old puffgut there with the pendulous mammaries. You've got the guilty party. Arrest her."

"Thank you for that corroboration, Secretary Goop."

Others on the tour had gathered around to watch the altercation in silence, as if it were a little show. The sergeant opened the morning *Observer* and consulted the list of new and revised ordinances. "Here we are . . . 'Inattentive walking in a temple and stepping on a sacred slug.' You'll do an indefinite at the Valdosta Colony."

ON BOARDING THE big orbigator, *Noctule*, for the two-day trip to Valdosta, prisoners were stripped and their old clothes incinerated. They were issued wooden clogs and tight-fitting jumpsuits lined with pig hide. The coarse bristles were sharp enough to irritate and chafe the skin but too dull to puncture it. Balance, Ophelia thought, picking splinters from her clogs before stepping into them. Everything in balance. Under an order of silence, the prisoners were marched into an assembly room for an orientation session.

"Heads up, all of you," the sergeant in charge said. "Day after tomorrow we'll be landing at Valdosta. As soon as you take possession of your run-down little reclaimed acre, you'll be given your mule, plow, other farming implements, and a working Stinker. Immediately have your Stinker grub out the undergrowth and sow a mixture of oats, lespedeza, sucker weed, orchard grass, and timothy. When this is done, set Russian mulberry trees in a shelter belt. They will grow to a height of two- to ten-hundred feet, control necrotic wind erosion, provide fence posts and fuel, and produce an abundance of berries, attracting thousands of birds, and all the grasshoppers will be eaten and shat, eaten and shat. What could be better than that? Any questions? You're no longer under a silence order."

"That awful smell," Ophelia said, "where is it coming from?"

"We've got a load of Stinkers on board, just below us. Workers. You'll be getting one, as I said."

"How do we manage them?" a prisoner asked.

"Easily. They dig holes or sleep under a pile of leaves in any weather. No need to feed them or clothe them. They'll manage that themselves. They'll forage. They'll bake and weave. And they're very good with mules. Now, let's all move toward the refectory. It's time to eat."

Ophelia contrived to get in line behind Mrs. Moldenke, who recognized Dr. Burnheart in the crowd and signaled him to fall in with them.

"What's your sentence?" he asked Ophelia.

"Killing a German in the French Sewer. And fetal theft of a neut. They said I felt strong urges to become pregnant and have a mixed-breed of my own, but I couldn't, so I kidnapped a neutrodyne female close to delivering. They said I took her to a secluded area, rendered her unconscious, and performed a cesarean section with a pocketknife. The neut was delivered alive, but the mother bled to death. Ridiculous, of course, but I didn't have a waiver. An uncle had given me one as he lay dying of a self-inflicted hammer blow to the head. I used it, though, and could never get another one."

"No sense in worrying," Mrs. Moldenke said. "A great Forgetting is on the way. All this will be gone."

"I'll welcome it when it comes," Ophelia said. "What sort of horrible crimes did you commit, Doctor?"

"Impregnating a neut gal. I didn't do it, of course. And you, Mrs. Moldenke?"

Mrs. Moldenke burbled with laughter. "Stepping on a temple slug."

The three sat together as neutrodyne servers rolled food carts into the refectory. Stopping at the head of each table, they ladled hot fungu into bowls and passed them hand to hand. A shaker of phosphate and another of root powder were left on the table for those who favored spicier fungu.

"I loathe fungu," Burnheart said.

Ophelia said, "It's earthy, like humus."

Mrs. Moldenke blew on her first spoonful to cool the fungu. "I like to let it harden a little before I eat it. They tell me it's packed with nutrients."

"You can count on a bowel movement right after eating it," Dr. Burnheart said. "It's disgusting stuff. I simply can't stand it in my mouth."

The sergeant in charge made his rounds, looking for any offense to punish or good deportment to reward. His flocculus was engorged, close to ripening, his wide-set, peglike teeth set on edge.

"Look at his flocculus," Ophelia said. "It's just about to burst."

"Please, Ophelia, don't do anything to attract attention. He'll see I'm not eating this stuff."

"Sergeant! Sergeant! Over here!" It was an American prisoner sitting behind Dr. Burnheart. "This man was complaining about the food. What does he want, green gland at every meal? I think he should be punished. Right here and now."

The sergeant wasted no time in getting to Burnheart, climbing over tables, knocking bowls of fungu everywhere. "What's the trouble here?"

"No trouble," Ophelia said.

The tattletale sang out. "That one. Complaining about the quality of the food. What nerve."

"Stand up, you ingrate."

"This is my third trip, Sergeant. My third sentence. Mind you, all the charges were spurious. I was never guilty once. It's time for some balance here. Surely, taking all that into consideration, you can see your way to overlook a moment of inappropriate carping. We have to avoid a *de gustibus* argument here. The same food that you neuts find tasty may be completely unappetizing, even revolting, to me. But who's to decide? Who's the arbiter of taste . . . especially in the mouth?"

"Sit down and eat, you lout. And no more complaining. I'll be watching you. Don't ever rest easy."

Burnheart dropped to his seat and lapped at the fungu.

After breakfast, prisoners were marched into the orbigator's capacious lavatory and allowed a generous period for toileting. Each was given a handful of edible paper for wiping, a small cake of caustic soda soap, a metal specimen pan, and a jar of depilatory.

"Remember two things, please," said the sergeant as prisoners went about their business. "One, every single hair must be removed. Close inspections will follow depilations. You come to Valdosta the same way you came to life, without raiment, without preconception, without worms, and without hair. And let me remind you again of what President Ratt has been saying until he's blue in the face—fight worms for a worm-free world. When your stool is in the pan, check it for movement, for tiny, almost unnoticeable encapsulations, for anything suspicious. If you see something, call me over for a look." The sergeant then went from prisoner to prisoner, poking through stool with a wooden stick, sometimes raising the pan for a diagnostic sniff.

Dr. Burnheart and Mrs. Moldenke, squatting side by side over their pans, conversed as best they could between grunts, gasps, strainings, and sighs of relief.

"I'm thinking of taking up deformation as a specialty," Burnheart said. "It's an art form, you know. The only form recognized and financed by the Ratt administration."

"All the best surgeons are doing it," Mrs. Moldenke said.

"I'll spend my entire time at Valdosta learning it, mastering it. Maybe I can practice on my Stinker. Then I'll study with Ferry in New Oleo. He sets the standard they tell me."

"Sometimes I fancy getting something done to myself," said Mrs. Moldenke. "But I'm a little too old for vanity. I'll stay the way I am."

Dr. Burnheart lifted a buttock and gave a push. Hearing the flop of his stool in the pan, he wiped, then knelt to examine it. To his dismay he saw a white worm, hair-thin, wound in a knot and struggling to untie itself. "Oh, bugger, I've got them. Sergeant? Over here!"

"Just a moment. Can't you see I've got my hands full?"

"Sorry, Sergeant."

When it came time to inspect Dr. Burnheart's specimen, the sergeant plucked the worm away from the stool with a small forceps, then held it up for all to see. "Attention, everyone! Attention! *Regardez!* This is the species you should all be looking for—*tubularia Vinkii*. It has two sides, as you can see, but only one surface. As yet, Valdosta is *tubularia* free. For the Ratt administration, it's a shining example of what stringent sanitary measures can do for a people."

"My vote is in his pocket," Burnheart said. "Fight worms for a worm-free world," Burnheart said. "I can believe in that."

"Top notch," said the Sergeant. "As soon as we land, you'll get a strong dose of vermifuge."

The sergeant examined Mrs. Moldenke's stool, then Ophelia's. "These look clean." He sniffed them. "Oh, yes. Very nice. No worms here." He moved along the line, sniffing pans.

A neutrodyne prisoner seated behind Mrs. Moldenke grunted, "My flocculus, it's fruiting. Why don't you Americans have a taste of green. It's harvest time."

"Suits me," said Dr. Burnheart. "That fungu wasn't exactly the cat's meow, not even with a lot of powder on it."

"I'd love some gland," said Mrs. Moldenke.

Ophelia blew a bit of froth from the corner of her mouth. "I'm drooling for some," she said

Using his fingernails, the neut tore open the rindlike outer skin of the flocculus, exposing a bite-sized, steaming green globe of meat. He held the flocculus out for Ophelia's convenience. When she bit into the gland, the neut swooned. "Ahhh . . . the relief. The calming. . . ."

The process was repeated for Mrs. Moldenke, who remarked, "Divine," and swallowed a mouthful of gland without chewing.

And again for Dr. Burnheart. "Ah, the best," he said, savoring it, letting it remain in his mouth until it melted away. "Even at the Pisstown Glandfest, there is nothing to compare to this. Nonpareil in every way. Prime stuff. Good green, sir."

The flocculus expelled a jet of air and retracted. "All gone for now," the neut said. "Americans, there's another lesson for you. Regardless of the law, you either eat the green when it ripens, or watch it shrivel and rot."

"It *could* be canned in quantity and sold," said Mrs. Moldenke. "Perhaps I should look into the possibility. There may be a profit in it. For you, for me. Edible paper was certainly a moneymaker for everybody."

"A heavy purse in a neut's pocket fast becomes a heavy curse," the neut said. "During the Chaos, remember, a kernel of wheat was more valuable to us than all the diamonds in Indistan."

"Suit yourself, I only thought—"

"*Scheiß!*" A German banged his fist on the table. "I vanted zum green!"

"Swearing is a superfluity of naughtiness," the sergeant said. "Don't let me hear it again. If I do, I'll bite off that tongue and nail it to your kraut head."

"Vat if I haff a vaiffer?"

"In that event, I'll nail it to the head of a bystander. Either way you lose a tongue. So I'd curb it now and save that waiver for later."

"*Danke.*"

"More than that. I trust you'll promise to heed the Arvian teachings from this day forward. Night and day you'll say, 'We'll watch and we'll wait . . . our lamps trimmed and burning. We know not the hour, we know not the day. We know only this: the next Great Forgetting is well on its way.'"

"*Yez, nacht und tag. Nacht und tag.*"

PRESIDENT RATT WAS enjoying a buffet luncheon at the Squat 'n' Gobble in Tesla Town when, across the street, an explosion at a guida factory left fifty neutrodynes with severe burns. Clouds of singed root-flour and hot poudrette fell to the sidewalk below. Neutrodyne workers and pedestrians, knowing no better, gawked at the spectacle and were blistered in the face. Some were blinded. One died of fright.

The President toured the ruins of the facility as soon as the fires were out. Gerald Hilter dogged him, firing questions. "Sir, fifty neuts burned. There were blindings, blisters, a death. What sort of action do you plan to take? This is the third 'accidental' explosion just in the month of Fruiting."

"What's actually more newsworthy, Hilter, is this. An energy-free cooling system has been installed in my office at the Rattery. A large brick vault was constructed in the basement below the room and provided with shelves of corrugated iron on which blocks of ice are placed, about a ton a day in the sunnier months. An apparatus forces the cold air blasts from the vault into the office over chloride of lime, which removes all dampness. The equipment controls the temperature during the hottest days to a degree that I and my assistants always find comfortable."

"That's very nice, sir, but . . . the deplorable working conditions in the hair mills, the mulce camps, the bakeries, the money plants. The workers are restless and the voters are wondering."

"Making money is a risky business, Hilter. There's your headline. Now to the meat of things. People overlooked the positive side of the Big Shift. The excitement and energy these relocations produced. The economic benefits alone were staggering—a redistribution of financial assets, new business incentives, no more stagnation and pooling of guida. But the greatest benefit, frankly, was that no one ever lost hope. You could be washing tripe in Pisstown one day, and the next day be fishing plesio off the coast of Holly Island."

"Thank you, sir, for speaking to the point."

"Honesty is my major protocol, Gerald. I'm telling it like it is now."

"Of course, sir, it often went the other way. One could be down-shifted."

"Yes, fortunes lost, great romances ended, all by random selection, a lottery to be exact, and it makes everyone potentially equal with everyone else. Finally, the American dream will come to pass. By the back door, but at least it will come to pass. Before the Forgetting we hope."

"And in the middle of the Big Shift, you introduced—"

"That's right. Legal microsystems. The idea was, and it seemed radical at the time, to say to these displaced populations—go ahead, take the law into your own hands. Form street-level judiciary districts, write your own laws, elect your own judges and juries, and yes, even carry out your own punishments. You hang them in the park and everyone has a picnic. It's really a simple concept. Imagine, there we were, in the age of Sinatra, extolling the virtues of the status quo. I say constant change is the answer, dizzying change. Upheavals of every kind. I take my inspiration from the Great Forgettings, all twelve of them."

"There were twelve? I didn't know a number had been arrived at."

"Oh, yes. What we don't know is how much time elapsed between them. Was it a lifetime, three lifetimes, or just a few ticks of the clock? Ten new moons or a short winter's day? Nor do we know when the Forgettings began."

"Some think they originated with the death of Arvey, during the time of Sinatra."

"Perhaps that is true. Perhaps it is not. No one can remember."

"They say the bolt of lightning that struck you when you were golfing left you with such a palsy in your writing hand, you couldn't so much as sign a waiver for the longest time."

"True. But I've recently taken up the pen again, this time to write verse. I'm working now on a poem that will have the power to kill, if read aloud, and properly. Perhaps it would not induce mortality in a healthy specimen, but a sickly individual, yes, very likely. The rhythm is crucial, absolutely crucial. You make the words fall into perfect rhythm, a monotony—*then* you cut in suddenly with a violently discordant element and you just might shock the heart into failing."

"Thank you for your precious time, sir."

"One more thing. The Jing. Soon I will place this practice into mandatory law."

"The Jing?"

"Jing's what makes us immune to all the dreaded diseases. When we have orgasms we lose *jing*, which destroys the immune system. The correct number of orgasms varies with the seasons. I like none in the winter, then two or three a week in the spring. Fall and summer are devoted to prolonged sex with my neut gals, without orgasm, which builds up *jing* and produces a heightened state of the brain called the Energy of the Golden Stove. When I sex with my gals, my head must point north. The *jing* flows a lot better that way."

"Again, sir. Thanks for your time."

"Don't print any lies, Hilter. I'll personally unman you with my garden shears."

"Oh, no, sir. No lies.

Radio Ratt:

In an apparent act of self-sacrifice, a New Oleo neutrodyne chained himself to a greasewood shrub with a onety-five-foot logging chain attached to a twoty-inch metal collar around his neck. Thirty days and nights later, a gibnut hunter found his bones in the thicket, along with evidence that the neut had nourished himself only with what palmetto leaves and bark he could reach. The hunter also found a crude toilet, which the neut had dug into the cold, hard earth with an entrenching tool, and a note to President Ratt, written in spew. The contents have not yet been revealed.

NEAR THE END of the ninety-ninth day of Moldenke's term in the sewer, Superintendent Montfaucon drew up to him in a two-man pedalboat. One of the seats was empty. "My friend, Moldenke. Turn in your tunic, your boots, and your *rabot*. Your sentence is over. Word's come down."

"Thank you, sir. That's a great relief. Just that sudden, eh? Not a bit of warning."

"Using Ratt's guidelines, prisoners are released in random fashion, much the same way they were arrested in the first place."

"Makes sense," Moldenke said. "Everything in balance."

"Correct."

Though Montfaucon was strangely oblique in his thinking, dangerously impulsive, and given to violent episodes, Moldenke was cognizant of the fact that on his watch, sewer conditions had become more humane. There were new rubber mattresses for the dormitory beds, a cold-water shower room, increased allotments of fungu, occasional meals of green gland, even a bakery.

"Thank you very much, Mr. Montfaucon," Moldenke said, "for your tireless efforts at improving the lot of us prisoners."

"No encomia are necessary, Moldenke. Get into the boat. We'll pedal to the exit. The rest of the way is against the flow. Prepare to pedal hard."

Moldenke climbed down into the cramped little vessel and strapped his feet to the pedals.

"After this, I vow on my mother's grave to get a waiver. It's the only way to stay on the straight and narrow."

Montfaucon said, "Here, there's a big clump coming. Break it up as we go by."

Moldenke held the *rabot* firmly and thrust it against the irregular clump's crust only to have it slip from his grip, bounce back, and strike Montfaucon in the midsection, taking the wind out of him.

"Sorry, sir. It was a bad bounce."

Montfaucon drew his pistol. "I killed a lot of Americans in the Chaos and I won't hesitate to shoot an ignoramus like you. I didn't say to harpoon the thing. I told you to break it up."

"Again, I'm sorry."

"Are you an Arvian? You better be. Don't you know they're bringing him back."

"I'm an Arvian all right. Can't wait till they bring him around."

Montfaucon put away the pistol. "We'll be making a stop just ahead."

Not far from the Sewer's exit, where the daylight shown in, the new bakery came into sight. "There you have it, Moldenke. Now every prisoner will enjoy fresh johnnycakes with his fungu."

Moldenke smelled baking dough and felt the heat of the ovens. "My compliments, sir. It looks like a fine installation. Floor to ceiling, steel and glass. Very nice. Just looking at it, I get goosebumps."

"And when the tour boat comes by, all the baking activities can be plainly seen. Generations will benefit."

There were ten or onety-two prisoners working in the bakery, some feeding bricks of *poudrette* to a stone oven, others kneading dough, some giving the johnnycakes their characteristic half-moon shape.

Montfaucon said, "Stop pedaling! *Arrêt!* Stop the boat. I'm going in. You come with me. I want to show you what it takes to run a good *boulangerie.*"

After guiding the boat into a small slip in front of the bakery, Montfaucon ran as fast as his hammy legs would carry him to the entrance, paused long enough to display a two-handed "thumbs up" gesture for Moldenke to see, then stormed in. Through the windows, Moldenke watched him slap a settler woman hard in the face before pushing her to the ground.

"Please, *monsieur.* Please!" The woman's tunic had come open during the fall, exposing ragged, stained underdrawers.

"Look at you, you dirty thing. You spit in the dough, I saw you."

"I did not, *monsieur!* I did not! It must have been an illusion." She struggled to button her tunic.

"An illusion? Are you suggesting that I am subject to some sort of—" He drew his pistol and placed the barrel between her eyes.

Moldenke strolled inside. Half-kneeling, he said, "Sir, I think the woman meant an *optical* illusion. A reflection in the glass, perhaps."

"He's right, *monsieur*. I wouldn't dream of spitting in the dough."

Montfaucon's hateful glare mellowed. The pistol was put away. "All right, Moldenke. I'll admit, it could have been a reflection." To the woman, he snapped, "Go back to work!" She leapt to her feet and began kneading dough again.

"What about the rest of you?" Montfaucon asked. "I want to see what you're wearing underneath. Show me." The workers obediently raised their tunics. Every pair of underdrawers was filthy and torn. Montfaucon pinched his nose with a thumb and forefinger. "Mother of God, this is not a bakery. This is a pesthouse! A septic nightmare! Tomorrow, everyone gets brand new unders. Several pair. The best available quality."

"Now that," Moldenke said, "that is an uncommonly large gesture, sir."

"Thank you, Moldenke." He drew his pistol and shot the worker standing nearest him, the bullet entering the man's skull just above the left ear. He did not fall immediately, but took a few steps in the direction of the oven, then sank to his knees, feeling his head for the wound. Montfaucon followed him and fired a second bullet into the back of his neck. This time, the man fell to the floor with a thud.

"Balance," Montfaucon said. "Everything in balance. I tend to agree with Ratt on that. Life . . . death . . . what's the difference? Two pickets in the same fence. You agree, Moldenke?"

"*Oui, monsieur*. I certainly do. That's definitely in the affirmative."

Though the fatally wounded bakery worker's fingers twitched, there were no other signs of life. One eye was open, the other shut.

Montfaucon winked at Moldenke. "Before you leave the sewer, I've decided to show you something very few ever see. Come, come." The two followed a complex route through the bakery, squeezing sideways in narrow passageways behind ovens, ducking under conveyors, through a nondescript door that led to a narrow hallway, in turn offering a choice of several other nondescript doors. At the end of the hallway hung an Ophelia Balls portrait of Mrs. Moldenke, striking a stern, matronly pose.

"She's something of a saint around here," Montfaucon said. "And it's because of her that I'm letting you in here."

Moldenke could hear the clatter of machinery, the buzz of prison workers conversing. "The bakery extends quite a ways, doesn't it," he said.

"*Non, non.* This is not the bakery." He opened one of the doors. "This is where edible paper is made . . . for money, for waivers, for wiping, for books. Your mother and me, in partnership. It's one of our bold new concepts. Prison industry."

They entered a cavernous room where prisoners were shoveling dry *poudrette* into vats while others, standing in the vats, mixed in buckets of sour mulce. The paste-like result was transferred to the bed of a steam press, which stamped each load into a sheet of paper. Workers then passed the sheet through a bleaching agent bath, misted it with lavender scent, and hung it to dry.

"Behold, Moldenke. You may have been her bodily child. But this is her brainchild. A perfectly harmonious system, all enclosed, entirely of waste, but which wastes nothing. You begin with sewer sludge, purified by secret processes until it is not only edible, but nutty in taste. You mix the *poudrette* with good fresh mulce, you press it, you bleach it. Voila! Nutritious, edible paper, with its many, many uses."

"Mother was ahead of her time. A true original."

"You're free to go, now, Moldenke. Let's pedal to the exit. And don't forget to shade your eyes. This long in unnatural light, the sudden brightness could blind you."

As they made their way back to the pedal boat, Montfaucon paused over the worker's body, said "Look there, both eyes open now. He isn't gone," and fired a *coup de grâce* into the forehead.

A tour boat floated past the bakery bearing a party of well-heeled neutrodynes from Indiana. Their guide offered commentary through a megaphone: "And here we have the newly completed baking facility, another example of Superintendent Montfaucon's progressive thinking. The fuel you see being loaded into these massive ovens is made from one hundred percent desiccated sludge, or *poudrette.*"

Montfaucon waved vigorously at the passing boat.

"Oh, look, there is Superintendent Montfaucon him-self!" the guide shrieked.

The neutrodynes applauded enthusiastically, one of them shouting, "Neuts for Montfaucon! You've got my vote!" The voice echoed up and down the sewer tunnel.

As Moldenke and Montfaucon stood at the exit gate, Montfaucon said, "You've not heard the news in a while, have you, Moldenke?"

"Not a whisper of it, sir."

"Then let me be the first to tell you. I've announced my candidacy for the highest office. I'll be going against Ratt."

"I didn't think that was possible."

"It is if you can swing the neuts to your side. . . . 'All unit-ed under Montfaucon!' That's my slogan. Remember that, Moldenke. 'All united under Montfaucon!'"

"Yes, sir. . . . All united under Montfaucon."

WITH HIS SENTENCE over and his mother off to Valdosta, Moldenke assumed responsibility for watching over the Moldenke mansion. While it was stately and large, the mansion was also shabby in certain ways, built with many eccentric architectural units and untrustworthy spaces. Whole wings were built completely out of square during the last Great Forgetting, left unfinished by disinterested carpenters, sloppy masons, and whimsical architects.

Before the Forgetting, they say, Dorothy Peters and her Stinker husband, Robin C. Heat, lived in the mansion while she served her eighty-year term as president. At that time it was remote from the city, surrounded by a hundred acres of orchard, vineyard, field, and range, along with a woodlot and a fishing pond. After the ravages of the Forgetting, the mansion was abandoned. Neutrodynes assumed possession of the property, and it quickly fell into disrepair. With no inclination toward sustained effort at upkeep on the part of the neuts, the roof eventually fell in and killed onety-three of them. Mrs. Moldenke then purchased the dilapidated mansion from the Michael Ratt Trust, which, under his control and direction, had subdivided the acreage into small lots and sold them to arriving settlers at enormous profit. By the time Mrs. Moldenke had completed repairs on the mansion, it was a walled-in fortress of less than three acres, encircled by a wide band of hastily built settler huts.

Now, with the mansion empty, and time on his hands, Moldenke determined to investigate the source of a low hum that seemed ever present in certain first-floor rooms during the day, always ceasing at nightfall. Since childhood he had heard it intensify from year to year, but whenever he'd mentioned this to his mother, who never entered the cellar, she dismissed him curtly. "You've got a ringing in your ears, son. Stop digging for wax with your fingernail."

Equipped with a fusel-oil lamp, gloves, and a burlap veil, he entered the cellar. His suspicions were confirmed. Bees had turned it into a tremendous hive. There was a great deposit of honey, a solid mass six inches thick, two feet wide, and fourteen feet high, extending from the cellar to the beams that supported the first story, then following the inside of the wall upward into the first-floor dining room. The bees were entering this storehouse through a knothole in an outside door.

Honey and comb being valuable commodities in the Bum Bay market, Moldenke was prompted to fill a bucket with them. But as soon as he began breaking off chunks of the comb, a corner of his veil got stuck in the sweet glue and flew from his head. He was so severely stung that by the time he had run to the camphor tree in the courtyard, his head had swollen three times its normal size. He lay prostrate in the hot sun for two days, feverish and unable to lift his head, soiling himself repeatedly. For sustenance, he managed to shovel a few bitter camphor berries into his mouth.

For months afterward he was insensate to the point that nothing bestirred his nerves or his passions. When sensation did return, it was invariably associated with a sharp discharge of the sacral plexus, causing his legs to buckle slightly, as if he were genuflecting. Worst of all, the hum of the bees, an enduring memento of the experience, would be a constant companion the rest of his days.

Fearing another such attack, Moldenke forsook all caretaking responsibilities, boarded up the mansion, and locked the gate. He dawdled lazily a few days in his room at the Adolphus, moved the room's furnishings from one place to another, smoked hair, and guzzled mulce.

Mealtime found him eating green gland at the Squat 'n' Gobble. "Where's all the gland coming from?" he asked the neut gal behind the counter. "The market bins are full of it, it's fresh, cheap. All the restaurants are serving it."

"There's always a big harvest before a Forgetting," she said.

"Is it a certainty, that one is coming?"

"Eat up. You can bank on it."

"Forgetting or not, I need work. Have you heard of any?"

"Customers say Zeus Bologna is taking on gland washers."

"I'll apply tomorrow. By the way, do you know where I can get a bale of hair? I'm out."

"Big shortage, I hear. The price is way up in the sky."

"Plenty of glands, very little hair," Moldenke said. "Everything in balance. I'm beginning to get glimpses of the big picture."

Del Piombo, walking with crutches, eased himself onto the stool beside Moldenke.

"Piombo."

"In the flesh."

"Crutches?"

"A little conflict with the law. They gave me fifty whacks on the shin with a billy club for farting outside the Rattery."

"What can I get you, Mr. Piombo?" the neut gal asked.

"A black egg omelet if you don't mind, no *poudrette*, and a mug of cold mulce."

"Back in a jiffy with that."

"Thank you, dear."

"I've been doing what you told me," Moldenke said. "Any further instructions?"

"Things are already in motion."

"Good. Good to hear that."

"You've been doing right well so far. We like your work. Precious few in this godforsaken hole can hope to display that kind of talent. You're a natural for this heavy, heavy task."

"Thank you. Thank you very much. What exactly would you like me to do?"

"Get a job."

"I'm applying at Zeus Bologna, first thing tomorrow."

"I can tell you this. I know Mrs. Enso, the gland team leader. She will demand you get a haircut. She doesn't want hair in the vats. The last time that happened, an American woman's blouse and jacket got caught in the machinery. When Mrs. Enso arrived she found the woman's scalp already severed completely, from her eyelids to the nape of her neck and ear to ear. Doctors reattached the skin and muscle to the skull, but onety-three barrels of ground gland had to be thrown out."

"I'll get a haircut before I go."

"Is the guida holding out?"

"I have quite a bit left."

"Here's more." Piombo gave him another wog of guida. "Spread the word. We're all uniting under Montfaucon." He shoveled in his eggs. "Get a watch. Time is of the essence."

"I will. I'll get one." Moldenke said, rising from his stool, "I suppose I should go get a haircut right away."

"Don't forget, it's President Kenny Day. Be careful out there."

"Righto," Moldenke said.

The moment he stepped out of the Squat onto Arden Boulevard, a rifle shot cracked like a whip in the dead air. Then another, and two more. The neighborhood surrounding the Squat was almost solidly Arvian-occupied and on this day they would be taking pot shots at pedestrians, sometimes killing them.

Moldenke took cover in a vestibule until the firing stopped, then very cautiously peeked out. Across the way, a thin young man in Arvey getup and mask withdrew his rifle into the fifth-floor's shadows. After a kill, the Arvians always took pause to meditate. Pedestrians could continue in reasonable safety for a while. A few bodies lay in the street near the bus stop, mostly Americans, sprawled where they were shot. Homeless Stinkers searched the bodies for anything of use or value. Moldenke joined them.

"Any watches?" he asked. "Seen any watches?" One of the Stinkers had a basketful.

"Take yer pick. Five guida. Taint no use to me."

Moldenke chose one with white hands and a black face. "Easy to see," he said.

Stopping at a bookroll kiosk before catching the bus to the barber shop, Moldenke selected an edible edition of Arvey's autobiography, *The Grassy Knoll*. "This one is cherry," said the vendor. "Very cherry. And all the spelling's been corrected."

"I'll have it on the pedal bus."

"Don't forget," the vendor warned. "The new ordinance. No reading on the buses. Strictly enforced. You must think only of pedaling. It's Ratt's newest whim, and things can get nasty if you're caught."

"We're all uniting under Montfaucon," Moldenke said, tentatively. "Spread the word."

The vendor shushed him. "Take care who you say that to, moron. You could end up hanging blue and bloated from a dead tree."

"Thank you for all the cautions," Moldenke said. "I'll watch my step."

On the way to the bus stop, he passed a great yawning well, the result of a land subsidence. Already neutrodynes had built stone steps leading down to the water's edge and were lined up in a row from the top of the steps to the bottom, each holding a chatty jar. One and all were engaged in the offices of the morning bath.

The brimming chatties were passed up and the empties down. The neutrodynes curried their legs, scoured their feet, polished their teeth with charcoal lumps, gargled, trumpeted their flocculuses, and hacked off their nails with kitchen cleavers.

One of the gals, shaving her flocculus with an old-fashioned corn knife, showed Moldenke a toothless grin. "Hey, you. Come down here. We've got a lot to talk about. Come on. Come down here. We'd like to talk to you. You won't be hurt. Please. Just come down the steps. The water is nice. We'll give you a bath. Come on, I'll sex with you. Be careful, though, the stones are sticky with slime."

Moldenke threw a handful of guida into the well. "Sorry. I'm in a big hurry." He backed away.

A chorus of voices floated out of the well:

"Come back, you!"

"Right now!"

"Come back here!"

"Come and be with us."

"Come on down. Plenty of fruiting glands."

"Cheap as dirt."

Moldenke turned and picked up his pace to the bus stop. Once aboard, he strapped his feet to the pedals and set the pedometer above his seat to zero. There were dozens of neuts climbing on, finding places to store bundles, strapping in, setting meters. It would be a while yet before the bus got going.

The temptation to read *The Grassy Knoll* was unavoidable. Moldenke could smell, even taste, the inviting, molasses-like sweetness drifting up from the bookroll. And if he held it in his hand much longer, it would be a sticky mess. All that considered, a little reading, he decided, might be worth the risk. Without further thought, he impulsively broke the paraffin seal, took the end-tab into his mouth, and began reading and eating as the roll unwound.

PART ONE
Portrait of an Assassin

I was a little fellow who liked to wear the pants. I spoke loudly to Marina, my wife, and didn't rise from my seat when I did so. I thought nothing of being harsh with her in front of guests and strangers, like an officer commanding a soldier: "Come here!" The way you call a dog. Once, I slapped her hard in the face for a half-zipped dress.

I ate fruit and sandwiches and drank milk, insisting the shades be kept down day and night. When I was thirteen, an elderly lady on a New York street handed me a leaflet about saving the Rosenbergs. I was moved to sympathy, and when they were executed I nearly fainted with rage. In the autumn of '55 I refused to salute the American flag before morning exercises at P.S. 117, the Bronx.

My wife said of me: "Sometimes it seemed he was living in another world, which he had constructed for himself, and he came down to earth only to go to work, earn money for family, eat, and sleep."

An obsessive overdresser, I was often observed even on summer days wearing a flannel shirt, woolen coat, suit, and atrocious-looking shoes made in Russia.

Of me a close observer has said: "A man of exceedingly poor background who read advanced books but didn't understand the words."

And another: "A wiry little runt who looked like a wasp—the menacing head at the end of a long neck, the mouth that moved independently of the face, the mechanistic body movements."

Clean-cut, impatient, arrogant, cold, inclined to be insolent, don't like dirt, don't like monotony, dictatorial, nervous, irritable, self-obsessed, logical, intelligent. That's me.

An old buddy says of me, truthfully: "He just wanted to be on the winning side for all eternity."

"All right, now, pedal harder, folks, or we'll never get there." It was the conductor, a neutrodyne, coming up the aisle, pushing the tip of his pencil into Moldenke's cheek. "No reading, imbecile! You expect the rest of the passengers to carry your weight? It's a turd like you that empties the pool of bathers."

"Punish him! Punish him!" shouted a fellow passenger.

The conductor, who had a head like a potato and a browned-over gouge for a mouth, thrust his face so close to Moldenke's, the tip of his flocculus bumped Moldenke's nose. "I could write you up and spank you on the spot," he said.

"Do it!" shouted another passenger. "Hurt him!"

"Excuse me, I don't mean to offend, or even to grovel," Moldenke said, "but when did neuts get to be conductors?"

"Bend over," the conductor scowled. "Take it like a man."

As everyone stopped pedaling to watch the action, the bus slowed and soon stopped.

Moldenke said, "I didn't mean to question your authority. It was perfectly legal yesterday . . . to read on the buses. And here we are, today, and it's a crime. Please, this a minor incident. Why make a stink over it? I don't need another brush with the courts."

"It's your job as a citizen to follow the changing statutes. Do you have a waiver?"

"I was told they were no longer available. That the Rattery had burned to the ground, that all the records were—"

"If that's the case, my friend, I'm a monkey's uncle. I was at the Rattery this very morning. All was well, and the line for waivers was moving briskly. I tell you what, I'll show some mercy. I won't write you up. . . . Now get down on your knees and eat the rest of that bookroll."

Moldenke knelt. "The whole thing? I'll choke."

"*Mange, mon ami. Mange!*"

Moldenke ate the bookroll an inch at a time as the conductor and passengers looked on. When the bookroll was eaten and the laughter had subsided, the conductor rang his bell and the pedaling resumed.

A sympathetic pedaler behind Moldenke leaned forward and whispered, "Remember the old days? When the neutrodynes were decent and pure? Breeding with us has made them better looking, but mean as the dickens."

"I couldn't be more in agreement," Moldenke said. At the edge of Sapodilla Park, he got off in front of Karl's Kuts, an administration-approved tonsorium, and took his place at the end of a line that snaked around the block. By the time he got to the chair, after an hours-long wait, his feet throbbed and his stomach ached. The bookroll was dissolving badly, producing a stinging acid reflux. Sometimes small, bitter surges of bile came as far as his mouth and had to be swallowed again.

Karl scrubbed his hands in a sink full of dirty water. He was a rosy-cheeked German with a single eyebrow that stretched entirely across his forehead. "You work out at Zeus too?"

"Yes, I start first thing tomorrow."

"Good for you. Working with gland?"

"Yes, under Mrs. Enso."

He began the task of combing knots out of Moldenke's hair. "I know the woman. A very strict sanitarian. Sends me a lot of business."

"I heard. No hair in the vats."

"I can distinguish, by my sense of touch, onety-five different diameters of hair. Yours looks thinner than average. It is false economy to economize on combs. Too many think anything they can run through their hair will do. Too often they groom with a rake of the fingers. You see, rough or jagged teeth in a comb can break the scalp, start little bleedings. If you can afford it, tortoiseshell makes an ideal comb, especially the antique Italian ones. The fact that eyebrows and eyelashes can be strengthened and made to grow thicker and longer is not generally known. Once each day, or at least three times a week, all the hair of the eyebrows and eyelashes should be pulled slightly, exactly a dozen times. This removes all partially or entirely dead hairs, enabling the new ones to appear, which are stronger. These are the methods I use to cultivate this eyebrow of mine. It was no accident of birth, but painstakingly tweezed into existence, weeded like a hill of tender pea shoots and treated with a porridge made of quince seeds and rose water." He had a closer look at Moldenke's scalp, turning him in the chair to maximize the light. "Your scalp looks dry and brittle and your hair is full of salty residue, as if you'd been at sea."

"Quite perceptive," Moldenke said. "It was a long time ago, though. Two or three, maybe onety-seven years, at least, aboard the *Titanic*. I forget."

"Wash more often. Use a stiff brush and caustic soda. Mind if I smoke? I've been addicted to hair since my service in the Unguent War. The habit was quite widespread in the French-occupied areas, where I fought for a time. Initially, the odor of the smoke made my blood freeze. It seemed like a form of cannibalism, once removed. But I soon was a frequent user." He took up his clippers. "You must realize that my clippers and scissors are very dull after cutting hair all day . . . and my hands are quite numb. So I may have to be a little rough with you. They make us mow it so close these days." He touched Moldenke's chin with the tail of a comb: "Look at that little blue lump."

"Little blue lump?"

"Oh, yeah. I hate to tell you, but you've got a flocculus coming in. Been in close contact with neuts? Got ahold of some bad gland? Ever sex with a neut gal?"

"Well . . . yes. And suffered torments on both counts."

"That's all it takes, brother. In Americans, these growths are very, very infectious. That thing's going to get a lot bigger. Mrs. Enso won't have you, either. It's happened before. They go bad, they burst, they spill, they spoil a whole vat of gland. I'm telling you, my brother had one that hung all the way down to his navel. Eventually, the poor sucker had to go out and build himself a shack in the woods. Nobody'd go near him. Talk about a pariah."

THE NEXT MORNING Moldenke went for a look in the mirror. There had been an overnight spurt of growth, and around the base the flesh was changing color slowly, like a dying greasewood, from greenish to yellowish and on toward crimson. In succeeding days, he began to grow a beard, though he doubted his taut, undernourished flesh would yield a growth long and thick enough to hide even a moderate flocculus.

He wrote to his mother with the shocking news.

She replied:

> Dear Son,
>
> Give that flocculus a general overhauling about once a week. You'll grow fond of it like your father did. He called his Rory, as if it were his child. First, he shaved it with a good sharp razor and lots of cream. Then he cleaned out the opening—if you have one yet—with alcohol and a fine brush made of duck feathers. Then he soothed any eruptions with salt solution and sealed them with fusel-oil jelly. In a few months we were getting enough green gland to pickle for the winter. Let's hope yours is a producer, too.
>
> Carry on, Son. Back to my chores.
>
> I'm yours,
> Mother

Radio Ratt:

Ferry, famed New Oleo deformist, has created a new type of gibnut. For one, it is a team of two, but for another, it is a beast which, though it be two, is as one. The treated gibnut, with two heads, mated hind-quarters, and a single tail, is all energy without restraint. As amusing and useful as the animal is, Ferry cautions, if aroused, the heads will bite. . . . Inventor

Vink unveiled his Michael Ratt balloon today outside the Bum Bay orbigator station to the delight of hundreds. The giant balloon, as tall as the Rattery itself, was filled with a volatile gas vapor. Despite all precaution, its maiden voyage foundered when the gas-filled head caught fire and spewed burning chunks of waxed canvas over onlookers and into the French Sewer near Ice Palace Boulevard. Eighty died. President Ratt wired condolences from the Rattery. Work has already begun on a second, even larger, balloon. It is hoped the new balloon will be finished by Inauguration Day.

WHEN SLEET MONTH came, Moldenke was in a panic. His lower lip had begun to sag under the weight of the growing flocculus, exposing rotted teeth and bleeding gums, his beard too wispy and thin to hide it. About the middle of Ice month, it took a dramatic turn when a patch of scaly white crust, oval in shape, formed on the upper, most visible, part. At first he determined to leave the crust alone, not to prod at it, poke it with a pin, or even scratch it. But this restraint wasn't long in place before he impulsively used his fingernails to pare away a portion of the area, causing the flocculus to split open and seep fluid.

One morning he stood in front of the mirror and moved his head quickly. The flocculus swung like a pendulum. He tied a towel around it and went to the Squat 'n' Gobble.

"Why the towel, Moldenke?" the neut gal asked. "Got a flocculus?"

"Yeah. Can't get on at Zeus. They're worried I'll contaminate the gland vats."

"I hear they're hiring out at the fusel camps."

"I've been to every one. I've been everywhere."

"Have it removed, you fool."

"They come back even worse I'm told, in Americans." He lifted and moved the flocculus to the side so he could sip his mulce.

In a few days the flocculus hardened, became extremely painful to the touch, and began to look gangrenous. Having it removed, no matter the risk, was now a strong consideration.

As he sat pondering the question, there was a rumble in the hallway, the slop collector. He opened his door to find the filth-covered Stinker, wearing only a jockstrap and a hernia truss, humming "Back Home in Indiana." Beside him, on a wheeled cart, was a drum labeled SLOPS. A fuming hair cigarette, rolled with a guida note, dangled from his lower lip.

"Gimme yer slops, Dinky."

Moldenke gave him his slop bucket. The Stinker dumped the contents into the drum and knocked the bucket against the edge to get that last little bit. Passing the bucket back in, he said, "Thanks for a generous contribution, friend. But if I was you, I'd go fast as my legs'd carry me and see a doctor. You got worms in your stool the size of my little toe. That there flocculus o'yours is fixin' to hatch, son."

"It's a bad one. I know it."

"Remember the sanitary code, pal. Fight Worms for a Worm-Free World. You're s'posed ta go thru it ever' day lookin' fer worms. Hell, it's an order straight down from the president. He don't cozy much to people that let their flocculuses hatch. Better take steps, Mack." He wiped his forehead with a filthy rag. "Well, I guess I'll get on back to my work."

Moldenke had another look in the mirror. Yes, he could see movement in his flocculus. He took a deep drag on his last hair cigarette. In a resulting coughing fit, he spat something into his hand, a little writhing ball of thin, threadlike worms.

He flung them to the floor and looked into the mirror again, appalled by the unhealthy, greenish pallor of his flesh.

Unsteady on his feet, clinging to a rickety banister, he descended the stairs into the lobby wearing a homemade paper sunhat. He rang the desk bell and waited, sweeping up a fat, green fly with a quick movement of the hand. He pinched it until it popped between his two thumbs, and dropped it into a bowl on the counter.

Mr. McGory, the hotel custodian, was busy in a dark corner harvesting some of the fungu bulbs that were growing from the lobby's damp floor, cutting them up with scissors and putting the pieces into a basket. "That's right, Moldenke. Fight Flies for a Fly-Free World. Do your duty. . . . Oh, you've got a flocculus on the way." He lightly pinched Moldenke's flocculus with a dirty, arthritic finger. "You should have that one taken off. It'll go ripe and burst, you know."

"I know."

McGory sniffed at a handful of fungu. "Go see Dr. Ferry. He has new clinic in the Parkla Hospit."

"I thought he was down in New Oleo."

"A seaport town. Shiploads of settlers docking there every day. It was getting to be bedlam. And then the Stinkers came, and when the Stinkers came, Ferry packed up his practice and came here. He's the best deformist in Bum Bay already."

"That's the man for me," Moldenke said. "I'll see him right away."

"Take the Nth Street bus to Dilly Plaza, then go west by foot, past the Depositorium and over the old freeway, and you'll be at the Parkla. It's quite a nice old place. Very well-preserved mummies were found in the basement, probably left to molder there after the Great Forgetting of Zero Ten. Better hurry. You can count on the buses being full today. Big Ratt rally downtown. I just saw his new balloon above the Rattery. You *are* against Ratt, aren't you, Moldenke? You *do* back the Montfaucon candidacy, do you not?"

Moldenke shrugged. "A very loyal supporter. He's my man."

"Tell Ferry I sent you. He gives me a small commission for every patient I aim his way. Have I ever shown you what he did for me?"

"Not that I remember."

McGory unzipped his jumpsuit. "He gave me a working dug." The mulce-swollen dug had been sewn in a few inches beneath the base of McGory's neck. "I can drink some whenever I want." He lifted the dug and rubbed the nipple until mulce squirted into his open mouth. "And it didn't cost me an arm and a leg."

"I'm on my way," Moldenke said.

"Have him do something for you. Why go around like you do when it's hardly necessary any more?"

"I'll give it some thought."

It was a bright, hazy, cold day. A fine red dust filtered down through the air. Waiting for the bus, Moldenke scratched at the flocculus and tapped his foot on the pavement. A filthy Stinker appeared with a sack of dried green gland. "Help me. Buy some gland."

Moldenke pushed a guida note into the cup. "Looks like a good batch."

An American settler in a moldy business suit joined Moldenke at the stop. "Quite a flocculus you've got there," he said to Moldenke. "That's nothing. Take a look at these eyes." He closed his *Observer*, removed his dark glasses, and looked skyward. "It's a Ferry job. Ever see anything like it?"

"What are they?"

"French pig." The eyes filled their sockets and leaked tears that attracted sawflies. "My vision field is much wider and I'm filled with a feeling of wildness when I look at the world. Thank the stars we have Ratt in there. Deformation is here to stay. Are you a Ratt man?"

"All the way," Moldenke said.

"A whole lot of us will be shoveling *scheiß* if Montfaucon wins."

"Unthinkable."

"Go see Ferry. He's running French pig specials right now. Testicles, kidneys, hearts, I don't remember what all. It's the very latest thing."

"I'll ask about that."

"Those pig nuts will click loud in this town."

"Uh-huh."

Having circled the block, the Stinker appeared again. "Help me. Buy some gland."

"Don't patronize Stinkers!" said the pig-eyed American. "Haven't you read the paper?"

"I'd very much like to, but—"

"Don't patronize Stinkers. They are a certified curse on the land."

"You want some gland, mister? Or not?" The braided twine handle of the Stinker's gland basket cut deeply into the degraded arm. A thick tan blood crept down the handle into the glands. "I have my rounds to make."

"Take your glands and go," Moldenke said.

The Stinker scuttled off, leaving its earthy scent behind.

The bus rumbled around the corner and coasted to a stop. The conductor stood in the doorway. "Only one. One seat open only."

"You go," said the deformed American. "I've got all day . . . and a new world to look at."

"Take care, then," Moldenke said, using the handrail to pull himself into the bus.

"I don't like what I see there," the conductor said, "those twitching legs and that swaybacked stance. Can you pedal hard enough to carry your own weight?"

"It's a nerve condition, not muscular. I can pedal with the best."

"Don't let that flocculus burst on the bus."

"Nothing like that. No, that won't happen. I'm on the way to have it removed."

"Take a seat, then. It's way in the back. Right behind those neutrodynes. Watch your step."

As Moldenke inched sideways past the neutrodynes, one of them said, "Hi, there, fella. Listen to this. I've composed a poem inside my head. It's called "The Death Egg," and it goes like this—"

The neutrodyne's companion said, "It's very catchy. Just listen."

"Clear the aisle!" the conductor shouted. "Don't make me come back there and stomp all over your skinny rump."

The neutrodyne tugged at Moldenke's sleeve. "Hear me out. It's a short one. "The Death Egg," by Erroll Dark. You get an egg, you gotta lay it. Like me mummy used to say it. You're a goner, sure enough, but at least you—"

The conductor's tone was threatening. "You neuts let that man by and start pedaling. If you don't, you're gonna be laying some eggs yourself when I get finished with you."

The neut let go of Moldenke's sleeve. "Your loss, American."

His companion said, "It was a work of art. The finish was terrific."

When Moldenke finally found his seat and buckled the pedal straps around his clogs, he looked up to see Ophelia Balls sitting opposite, her face partially hidden by an edible book entitled *Bubble Gum.*

"Ophelia? Back from Valdosta already?"

When she lowered the book, Moldenke was both shocked and comforted to see a flocculus budding on her chin. He knew that females only got them when they spooned with breeding neuts, a repellent thought, but his misery was glad for company. Though he treasured Ophelia's friendship and wit, when it came to sexing he was addicted to neuts and had no attraction for settlers. He was also confident that her sexual leanings matched his.

"Moldenke. I almost forgot about you. That's a rough-looking flocculus you're getting, a lot bigger than mine. Yes, I'm back from Valdosta. A blanket pardon came down from the Rattery."

"Lucky you. I paid my debt in the Sewer. I hear there's good air at Valdosta and potable water."

"In a way, I hated leaving. Very bucolic." She tore out a page of the edible and chewed it. "But we were all getting these." She touched the tip of her flocculus. "I'm going to Parkla to have it taken off."

"Me, too. Mine's about to go ripe on me."

"They say they grow right back sometimes."

"Some do, some don't. It's fifty-fifty."

"I'm sure they'll be keeping us there a day or two, so I'm bringing along Ratt's newest edible to read. It's the most flavorful thing he's ever written. Not much slush. Very little dullness. The scenery comes and goes. The characters move around doing things. And the dialog slides along with a pleasing swiftness. One of the characters says, 'You Americans put so much stock in the Forgettings. Forget it,' he says. 'Nothing matters,' he says, with emphasis on the nothing. It's a recurring theme. Nothing matters more than anything. Don't you get it? Have you read it?"

"Have I read it? Well, no, not yet. I'm very busy these days, working for Piombo."

"Doing what?"

"Oh, just going about my business. He has a plan. Somewhere along the line, I'll be tapped. It hasn't been specified what it is I'll do yet, or the nature of the plan."

"If you read the papers, you wouldn't go near that man. He's been implicated in some kind of plot. I don't remember." She rubbed one of her sore ankles. "It's only when I get on a pedal bus that I regret having had this leg job done. My feet don't fit the pedals right. It hurts so much my toenails bleed."

The conductor rang his bell. "Pedal harder, people. There's a lot of inertia to overcome."

Rarely oiled, the noisy, rusted pedal chains clanked into motion and there were the sharp reports of rifle shots as the bus pulled away. Through the broken rear window Moldenke saw the deformed American fall. In a few seconds, Stinkers had stripped him naked and carted off his clothes.

"It isn't President Kenny Day again already is it?" Moldenke asked.

"It could be." Ophelia scratched her head. "I can't remember."

When the bus gained enough momentum to make the pedaling easier, Ophelia went back to eating her way through *Bubble Gum*.

"I don't recommend that," Moldenke said, "unless you have a waiver. Brand new ordinance. No reading on the buses."

"Oh, that's been reversed. Look around you. As a matter of fact, reading is required now."

Moldenke surveyed the bus. Every passenger was reading something—edibles, pre-edibles, the *Observer*, Ratt's

Manifesto, The Grassy Knoll, The Poetry of Sincay Baxter.
"And here comes the conductor," he said, resignation rattling his voice.

"Don't worry," Ophelia said, reaching into her pigskin satchel. "I've got waivers." She offered Moldenke one. "Just off the presses."

"I know the trick. Vanishing ink. I'll be in worse trouble."

"Who's not reading there!" Perspiration drizzled from the conductor's mustache. "Something told me you'd be trouble when you got on, you stupid Indiana bastard. If this isn't the worse example of . . . I'd love to shovel something with spikes up your bean gun the wrong way."

"I beg your pardon."

"Well, you won't get one. I'm going to hail a sergeant at the next stop and put you in his custody. There's a significant punishment attached to this offense."

"Civil death," Ophelia said. "It was all over the papers, it was on the radio. All your rights are peeled away. You live entirely outside the law. Most of the civil dead head for the Stinker camps."

"Fair game," the conductor said. "Everybody's aiming for you. Somebody cuts out your guts with a corn knife, they can go to the Rattery and get a medal and handful of waivers."

"He has one," Ophelia said, placing a waiver in Moldenke's hand.

"Let me see that." The conductor examined the waiver, touched the tip of his tongue to the ink and tasted it. "Hmmm. Well . . . it looks like the genuine article. You're off the hook I suppose, but I warn you, the next time you get on a bus, read!" He tore the waiver into several shreds, rolled them into balls, and swallowed them like marshmallows.

When the conductor was out of earshot, Moldenke exhaled the breath he'd been holding and patted Ophelia on her shoulder. "Thanks for saving me."

"My pleasure. Here, read this before he comes after you again." She gave him a tattered, pre-edible pamphlet, *Sexing with Neuts: The Myths and the Facts.* "I'm giving thought to mating with one. If it takes, and there's an infant, I'll need better dugs. The ones I have are as dry as a mummy's. As long as I'm going in with this flocculus, why not have Ferry give me a good set of mulcing dugs?"

"Why not?" Moldenke agreed. "I've just seen a working one in action."

When the bus reached the end of the line at noon, there was a pale sun at midheaven. Moments after Moldenke and Ophelia got off, the sky darkened and a cold, rust-red rain began.

"I haven't heard any shots," Moldenke said.

"In quite a while," Ophelia said. "The Arvians must be meditating."

They hurried along President Kenny Boulevard, past the Ice Palace, where the slap of the paddle and the joyful shrieks of a youthful crowd echoed through Dilly Plaza. At the Depositorium, workers were tuck-pointing old, crumbling bricks and a Closed for Restoration sign hung across the entrance.

Ophelia sighed. "I so wanted to see the fifth-floor exhibit. The cartons of pre-edible books, the rifle, the gibnut bones from his last lunch. Apparently, he was working in the building at the time, making educational bookrolls."

"Funny," Moldenke said. "My sacrum discharges every time I walk by this place."

"It's an energy sink," Ophelia said. "I feel it, too. Like walking in mud. I'm light-headed."

Climbing over the Grassy Knoll, they headed for the Old Ruby Trail. From this vantage, they could see Parkla's upper floors jutting above a thicket of camphor trees and sucker weed. A few minutes' walk along the trail brought them to an encampment of homeless neuts, all males, who were roasting green glands over a smoldering pile of *poudrette*.

"Hello, strangers," one of them said. "They call me Spanish Johnny. Have some pickled plesio and some roasted glands with us."

"No time," Moldenke said. "Bad flocculus. Going to Ferry to have it removed."

"And I'm getting mulcing dugs," Ophelia said.

Spanish Johnny spit into the dirt. "Nothing is more vulgar than haste. Those blessed growths might look bad to you, Americans, but believe me, you're going to sorely miss them when they're gone." He threw a stone at a Stinker sitting around the fire. "Nephrastus, come on over and pleasure these settlers with a good story."

The Stinker stood unsteadily, coated with dust and dry leaves. A cluster of hard, black fecal pellets rolled out of his trouser leg. "OK, boss. Here's the story. I smoked sawdust behind Zeus Bologna and performed onanism in an apple for want of a natural opening. I fell asleep, dreaming I was at the head of a band of devils storming Indiana. I flung a burning *Manifesto* at a man's head, emptied a chamber pot onto a bed. That's when the drumming began: A rat. A tat. A ratta tat tat. There was a terrible fire at the Squat 'n' Gobble. Seven burned. Another crushed by falling timbers. And I'm on the scene, drumming for the dead. Rat a tat. Rat a tat. Rat tat tat a rat a tat, a rat tat tat, a rat tat tat. Going up and down the country after that. Rat tat tat. Rat tat tat. From eight till four in the morning, with a rattling, thundering noise. A rat. A rat. A rat tat tat. A rat. A tat. A ratta tat tat. People inquired,

'What is it about you, that you want to go all over the place going rat, a tat, a rat tat tat? Are you a witch? You're actually shaped like a drum.'

'I do have unlucky days,' I said in reply. 'My name is Nephrastus. My beat is the fastest.'

'No more drumming, you hear?' they said. Then Ratt came to town. An honor guard of plume-hatted Arvians drew up to see him lay the cornerstone of their new temple, watched him smooth the first applications of mortar with a silver trowel, watched him rise when he heard the sound. *Ooom pa pa. Oom pa pa. Oompa oompa Oompapa.* And he wondered what it was, going, *Oompapa Oompapa.* Was it a tuba or a man? Going *Oompa Oompa Oompapa. . . .*"

"Please," Moldenke said. "I'm begging you. No more. We have to get to Parkla."

"Be on your way. We have no use or liking for your kind," said Spanish Johnny. "Your mind will change when the Forgetting comes."

Nephrastus said, "Look! Ratt's balloon."

The great balloon, as big as a building and full of gas, floated just above Dilly Plaza, rotating slowly in a lazy breeze from the Firecracker Sea. It bore a passing resemblance to Ratt's head and shoulders, though the facial features had been brushed on in soluble black paint and were dissolving in the humid night air.

Radio Ratt:
A ghostly ship has been sighted by head-diggers off Diego Point, in blowing weather only. The stronger the wind, it seems, the more often the ship appears. Though the mist-enshrouded vessel is seen sailing at an immense rate before the wind, under full press of canvas, even in the most violent gales,

she is never known to go into port. Among head-diggers, the story goes that the captain of the ship and all its passengers have been condemned to beat about the sea since the last Great Forgetting. Ghost ship or not, head-digging continues on Holly Island at a feverish pitch. A rich mine of them has been found there, some still frozen, and diggers are pouring into the area in hopes of growing wealthy. In addition to the heads, many tons of healing unguent cream, valued at more than eight-zil guida, have been unearthed thus far.

ARRIVING AT PARKLA, Moldenke and Ophelia were greeted by a weatherbeaten sign above the entrance that read Virtue Never Dwelt Long with Filth.

They rested on an old wooden bench in the foyer. For the better part of an hour, Moldenke dozed. In a dream he saw Arvey posing for an old-fashioned photograph near a wooden picket fence. He held a magazine in one hand and a rifle in the other. The woman behind the Kodak was an attractive young Russian. Moldenke sensed that she was Arvey's wife.

Ophelia prodded him awake. "Get up, Moldenke. Let's go. The Arvians have set up a gauntlet for us."

"You first," one of them said to Moldenke, pointing a rifle at him. "Go through it or I'll blow your head off. They don't call this weapon a 'man licker' for nothing."

Moldenke crawled through the gauntlet, poked in the ribs with rifle butts, spat on, taunted with shouts of "Long live Fidel! Revenge the Bay of Pigs!" When he came to the end, a wiry young Arvian with a serious nature and a tensely set jaw held out a straw basket. "Please, help bring Arvey back. Where is he when we need him? Give us all the guida you've got."

DAVID OHLE

Moldenke took out Piombo's wad and rolled it into the basket.

"Dunka, dunka, whatta hunka. You're an honorary Arvian now, buster."

A small choir of Arvians then chanted a short recitation of their Credo, the *Last List:* "Typing—already he was at work on his memoirs. . . . Crystal for watch—time is of the essence. . . . Job—to get money to send to Marina and the kids. . . . Bank account—to put what was left in. . . . Mail—a postal box was always handy. . . . Job—it was a very big thing. . . . Haircut—it helped get a job . . . . Library—one of his favorite pre-edible books was Kenny's *Profiles in Courage.* . . . Plug for radio—his ear on the world, it had to be working. . . . Haircut—this, too, is mentioned twice. . . . In the name of Arvey. . . . We know the hour, we know not the day. We watch and we wait. Our lamps trimmed and burning. We know not the hour, we know not the day. Oh, Arvey. Oh, Arvey. Be with us *now.*"

Ophelia passed through the gauntlet unassailed. All Arvians averted their heads and eyes. They were following Ratt's latest ordinance, applying to Arvians only—never look directly at a female settler.

"Can you tell us how to find Dr. Ferry's clinic?" she asked one of the Arvians.

Averting his eyes and lowering his rifle, he said, "I've never been there, but I think I know. See that archway? That sign that says No Necronauts Beyond This Point. Go in there, up a flight to the mezzanine, turn north into the south wing, then head east until you pass the custodian's closet. From there you'll see stairs leading to a sunken arboretum. Careful . . . they're riddled with rust and very unstable. Once down, follow the path marked D45-K. It snakes through a stand of camphor, then a plot of greasewood, and there you are. Ferry's clinic. Stay alert in the greasewood. They tell me there's a rabid gibnut in there, lost its fur, acting oddly, going in circles and foaming at the snout. . . . Now, please move on along. Others are trying to get through the gauntlet."

Following the complex directions, with a few wrong turns and time spent finding their way out of no-outlet corridors, they came upon the shirtless custodian sitting on a nail keg outside the closet, his neck shortened by deformist surgery, the thick, brutish head lying flush with the shoulders, fixed in position, facing backward. He held a mop standing on end like a spear and stared dreamily at a tray of cleaning agents, saying their names again and again, attempting to commit them to memory. "There's lye, there's muriatic acid, ammonia, oil of citronella. Lye, muriatic, ammonia, citronella." The litany of cleaning agents continued until he reached a natural stopping point.

"Excuse me," Moldenke said.

Ophelia said, "That's a really fine head job. It has the stamp of Ferry's work."

"Thanks. It is. An original Ferry. I thought it best, finally, to start seeing where I've been rather than where I'm going."

"Excuse me," Moldenke repeated. "We need to find Ferry's clinic."

"Holy bitchment. I can see why. That flocculus is a nightmare. Go right down the hall to the stairs, down the stairs, and across the arboretum. Watch out for that gibnut. It has the blind staggers. Don't let it bite you. It always goes for that handy little tendon behind your ankle. And watch you don't slip on the way to the stairs. I've just bent over backward to wax that corridor with pure carnauba and buff it till I was dizzy. It's like walking on mirrors in felt slippers.

"It's nice to see someone taking pride in their work, however menial," Ophelia said.

She and Moldenke carried their clogs and walked barefoot on the highly polished floor to the arboretum stairs, whose metal understructure was a true example of neglect—unpainted support braces dangling loose, some steps missing altogether. The climb down was perilous, and, once off the stairs, they saw a muddy bog standing between them and the clean, dry stones of the path. The light, filtered through a dome of yellow pre-Forgetting glass and a crust of gull droppings, gave the arboretum an eerie glow and the feeling of stillness before a storm.

"That's a gibnut wallow," Moldenke said. "Keep your eyes open."

Ophelia's nostrils flared. "What's that I smell?"

"Musk," Moldenke said. "The gibnut's close."

The path across the arboretum was far from straight, curving around gibnut wallows, winding back on itself to avoid patches of sucker weed, sometimes taking abrupt right or left turns for no discernible reason.

"It's taking forever," Moldenke complained, just as a sudden tug at one of the legs of his jumpsuit threw him off balance. "It's the gibnut!"

Losing all feeling in his feet, he toppled into a thorny greasewood patch and pricked himself mercilessly. Then, rolling out of that hazard, he only entangled himself in sucker weed, whose florets clung to his throat and forehead. One by one, like nuts from a tree, he plucked them loose, leaving rosy welts at the points of attachment. Amid these struggles, the gibnut made its escape and Ophelia was not to be seen. Moldenke called her name a few times and got no response. He continued along the path, which curved less and less, and the thicket thinned.

When he reached the terrazzo gallery at the other side of the arboretum, a little troupe of Stinkers was putting on a dumb show. Another sold green glands, and a particularly scurvy one stood beside a cobbled-together casket. "You wanna fuck a Stinker?" he said, pinching Moldenke's collar. "She don't smell a bit. Fresh as a daisy. Just died this morning. The worms got her."

"Not interested," Moldenke said.

"Its legal, you know. Starting today at noon. It was on the radio."

"Get out of my way, please."

The Stinker backed away, the hem of his long gray overcoat dragging on the ground.

At last, the door to Ferry's clinic could be seen at the very end of the gallery. In a small rotunda otherwise empty of furnishings stood a wooden pedestal with a copper bowl containing two plasticine tokens bearing the numbers three and eight. Moldenke picked up the three, then put it back and took the eight.

Green arrows painted on the floor led him into a waiting room, where a nurse sat at a small metal desk. She was on the frail and pasty side, unblemished except for a few blisters on her cheek and a ripe pustule on her chin. Ten or onety-one patients sat motionless, listening to the nurse's radio.

"Give me your token," the nurse said. She put it into a hopper with the rest, mixing them in with a wooden spoon, stirring them like a soup. "I'll buzz your number when it comes up. Don't forget it. Sit down. It's time for the news." Moldenke found an empty chair and dutifully listened: "*Candidate Montfaucon was locked up in the American Jail yesterday afternoon for treating the inhabitants of the mulcing cage to a lighted cigar. Montfaucon threw the cigar into a mound of straw, thereby terrifying the gals and starting a fire*

DAVID OHLE

in the cage. . . . And over Indiana way, Lars Renfro, an explorer whose career was greatly accelerated when he discovered the east pole in Indiana's fertile crescent, was drained until dead today by Bloodgood Cutter, a bloodletter, hired by Montfaucon's goons, a maid and a cabby, who are to stand trial and be executed. . . . Finally, the Sinatra-Age pleasure ship Titanic *sank today off Permanganate Island, taking crew and all but two passengers to their watery graves. The two survivors were the French showman Topinard and one of his prodigies, the neutrodyne giant Indole, whose natural buoyancy saved both himself and his master. 'I'm saddened by the loss of Skatole,' Topinard told Radio Ratt. Despite his able coaching, he said, Skatole never learned to swim, or even float."*

Poor Udo, Moldenke thought.

When the nurse turned off the radio, ceiling fans came to life, revolving by virtue of a complex network of leather belts going from one fan to another and then through a slot high in the wall to whatever source of power was turning them.

A buzzer sounded three times. After a pause, it sounded again, three times. The nurse looked around. "Number eight?"

"I just came in," Moldenke said. "All these people were ahead of me."

"Damn you, if you're number eight, come here."

He stood at the nurse's desk, leaning on its edge for support.

"What are you seeking here? Deformation?"

"Bad flocculus. Maybe worms." He pointed to his chest. "And my boosters are getting old."

"Sheep or pig?"

"Sheep."

"Very old, then. Pre-Forgetting?"

"I don't remember."

"Ferry's not a sheep man, you know. You'll get pig this time. The French have developed an exceptionally stout-hearted strain. The heart goes forever. Dr. Ferry uses nothing else."

On entering Ferry's examining room with the nurse, Moldenke was dwarfed by a life-size blowup of Arvey that covered an entire wall. Opposite, Ferry sat at a card table eating hot fungu. "It's all I can keep down any more," he said. His head and face were pale and hairless. Above his eyes were pasted two snippets of wooly carpet, a poor mimic of eyebrows.

"He wants you to take off the flocculus, Doctor Ferry. And a few other things."

"Worms and a bum implant."

Ferry was feverish, tongue swollen, yellow and protruding. His voice was a shallow, throaty croak. "I'll be with you in a moment."

"Eat the rest of that fungu, Doctor." The nurse stirred it for him. "You know what happens when you don't. Look, it's getting cold on you."

Dr. Ferry took up the spoon and ate. The swollen tongue and loose dentures made the process haphazard and messy, the fungu spilling down his chin and onto his smock.

The nurse led Moldenke to the examining table. "Lie here and relax. I'll be getting back to the other patients. You be a good boy, now. It won't hurt a bit."

Ferry finished his fungu, then turned his attention to Moldenke. "Feeling listless . . . anemic? Lapses of memory?"

"All that."

"Impairment of the power to use words?"

"Often."

"The lapses of memory. How long have you had them?"

"I don't recall."

"Seeing any worms in the stool?"

"If I look."

"Stand up. Show me the implant."

Moldenke struggled with a rusty zipper until it ripped free of the cloth and his jumpsuit fell open.

"Who did this work?"

"Burnheart."

"When?"

"Just before the last Forgetting. A lung had to go to make room."

"We're much better at these things these days. We use pig now. French pig. It only takes one. Not so invasive. We can leave the lungs in place. A few days rest, an infusion of nuxated iron, and presto, there you are, ready to walk a new body around. Would you like me to pencil you in for tomorrow?"

"The cost?"

"Very, very modest. Three zil guida. We're Arvian run and well endowed."

"And my worms?"

Ferry slipped a finger into Moldenke's sparse beard and parted it. "Look at those encystings. We're going to have to go after your condition aggressively. We have healing strategies to attempt, but no guarantees. Let me have a look at your testicles. Ah, see there. The worms are beginning to migrate down into your sack. I tell you what, we're running a special on pig sacks. I could sew you on a pair in no time. Completely worm resistant. Very high sperm production. You could be knee-deep in offspring, provided you sex with neut gals only. That's the caveat on these pig nuts. No sexing with settler women."

"No problem for me," Moldenke said.

"We'll do it. I don't like the looks of that sack of yours. We can kill the worms, but the damage is done. I'll tell my Stinkers to cut a pig with your name on it."

"And the flocculus?"

"It's well rooted. Those kind have a habit of coming back with multiplied ferocity. Why don't we strike a balance here? I'll just give it a good trim and shape it up some. Maybe lighten that deep blue color and leave it at that."

"If you say so, Dr. Ferry."

"I say so." He pounded the top of his desk and called to the nurse.

"Yes, doctor?"

"Take him to the depilatorium, and when he's through there, get him settled in his room and put him to sleep. Tell the Stinks to ice down a fresh sack tonight."

"Yes, doctor."

"And on the way, be sure he sees what I've been doing with Arvey." He coughed up a little kernel of hard fungu.

"Is Arvey here?" Moldenke asked.

"Right down the hall," the nurse said cheerily. "It's something everyone should see."

Arvey was displayed behind the glass of the old nursery, angled slightly toward the viewer, his restored head in such lifelike condition that there were bubbles of saliva clustering around his mouth. The rest of the body lay separate from the head, covered with a black cloth.

"Behold," the nurse said. She knelt and bowed. "We know not the hour, we know not the day. The head is alive. Ask it anything. It will respond."

"Anything?"

"Yes, anything."

"When did you compose the last list?"

The facial muscles twitched and the dry lips peeled apart. The voice was hoarse. "After arriving in New Oleo, April 25, l963, a Thursday, I rented a small apartment at 98 X-Alley, then composed a list of things to do: typing, crystal for watch, job, bank account, mail, job, haircut, library, plug for radio, haircut, job. Five months later, on October l4, when I registered at 1026 Beckly St. in Dilly Plaza, I used the alias O. H. Lee."

The nurse said, "One more. Ask it one more."

"Is it true that you killed President Kenny?"

"I didn't kill anybody. I work at the depository. I lived in Minsk and in Moscow. . . . I worked in a radio factory. . . . I liked everything over there except the weather. . . . I have a wife and some children. . . . What is this all about? I know my rights!"

"That's about as far as he goes," the nurse said. "Naturally, his followers want to know the rest of Arvey's story. Don't you?"

"More than anyone, I suppose."

"It's just a matter of time until Dr. Ferry has him fully animated. What his work will be, what his mission is, we do not know. You do accept Arvey, don't you? You do believe he'll soon be rising from that bed?"

"Oh, yes. No question."

"Good, now let's get you depilated."

The depilatorium proved to be a steamy room with seven or eight showerheads sticking out of the tiled wall at different heights. A mold had taken over the grout and every tile was outlined in brilliant green. Under each showerhead, on a shelf, was a bowl of depilatory cream.

"You're on your own in here," the nurse said. "Remove your clothing and leave it to be laundered. Rub yourself head to toe with cream, let it do its work, then shower off,

But don't get any on your flocculus. There are dressing gowns in there. I'll take you to your room when you're finished." She closed the door. Moldenke removed his jumpsuit, clogs, and underdrawers, padded barefoot across the cold floor, found a showerhead the right height and stood under it. A fizzing sound rose from the cream jar when he opened it and, after applying the cream as instructed, every strand of his hair dislodged and slid away from his body when he turned on the shower.

When the nurse showed him to his room, he was pleasantly surprised. The bed linen was clean, the mattress firm, and a gleaming sink ran warm water. The commode flushed, there were plenty of pre-edible *Observers* to wipe with and a bedside table held a lamp and a radio.

"Thank you, nurse. By the way, is there a patient here by the name of Ophelia Balls?"

"Wanted a set of mulcers?"

"That's her."

"She went into depilation right behind you."

"I'm glad to hear that. I lost her in the arboretum."

"Good night, now. I'll wake you bright and early."

Exhausted, Moldenke dragged himself into bed and tuned in the Vink Report. Vink was discussing his latest researches with Michael Ratt. "My experiments with planimals continue," he said, "but my pig plant remains a dream."

Ratt said, "Yet your endeavors taught you to use telepathy on neuts."

"I can now transfer thought to them at a distance of a furlong," Vink said, "the result of my study of the forces behind telepathy and hypnotism since onety-nine, during my exile at Valdosta, when I lived among people who made good beer from honey and urine. In this jungle setting, my psychic-animism was spawned and grew fervid, along with the conviction that I must go to Bum Bay and let my discoveries be known to you, Mr. Ratt."

"Thank you, Vink, for that confidence, but as I comprehend this, the thought transference takes place while you are enclosed in a specially constructed iron pyrite box. Correct?"

"Correct. And the neutrodyne subject is inside an identical box."

Moldenke fell asleep and dreamed that he saw the Michael Ratt balloon tethered above a grandstand during an inauguration ceremony. When the balloon burst into flames and settled on the screaming crowd, he awakened to a severe pain in his scrotal sack.

The sun's morning face shone in his mirror. For a moment, he thought it was his own face, gone soft, smooth and faintly pink. There were streaks of blood on the sheet, a metallic taste in his mouth, and surgical stitching on his chest in the shape of an "X." When he stood to walk, his feet were no longer numb. Passing the mirror, he glanced at himself, then stopped for a longer look. His new French pig scrotal bag was encased in iodine-stained bandages, as was his trimmed-down flocculus. There was a regular heartbeat, so strong that his entire torso thumped. His mind was clear and he felt vital.

"It went very well," the nurse said, stepping into the room with a clean jumpsuit, underdrawers, and his clogs. "The heart is working well and we expect you'll be ready to sex in a few days, after the bandages are off your new sack. And, before I forget, he gave you the lung of a neut boy."

"When did it happen, nurse? I remember listening to the radio. I fell asleep. I don't remember anything after that."

"That's what makes Ferry Ferry. No recollection whatsoever of the surgery. Do come to dinner tonight in Ferry's private suite. It's just past the janitor's closet and to the east. The doctor is very, very harsh when it comes to tardiness. Latecomers are likely to get a tongue lashing at the very least. We'll ring the bell at about seven. Come immediately."

AS MOLDENKE DRESSED for dinner, he breathed more deeply and less often than ever and his new heart beat strongly and rapidly. Numbed from navel to knee, though, his new testicles had yet to provide any sensation. Blood ran through him under good pressure and made his thinking sharp. He had no trouble following the nurse's directions and locating the janitor's closet.

"Going to that goddamned dinner, are you?" the janitor whined.

"In Ferry's private suite. Right over there."

"I'm never invited to these things. All I do is clean and polish. That's my life. One of these days I'm going to kill that man."

"The nurse said not to be late. Ferry has a hissy."

"Go, then. Go."

The nurse answered Moldenke's knock. "I hope you have a good reason for being late. He's in a stormy mood and a little drunk." She led him into the dining room. A long table was set with china, silver, and linen. The rest of the patients were already seated, including Ophelia. All were well scrubbed and in clean jumpsuits.

Seated on opposite sides of the table, Moldenke and Ophelia were able to converse for awhile.

"I got off the path. I couldn't find you."

"No matter. Here we are. And I'm feeling extremely fit and energetic, if a little numb in places."

"My new dugs are perfect." She lifted them with her hands and tightened her jumpsuit against them. "The nipples are nice and big. And look under the table. See what he did with my feet?"

Moldenke lifted the table cloth and peeked. "What a thing. They're sideways."

"You should see me waddle. It's cute."

Ferry entered in a tuxedo, stood at the head of the table, and lit a hair pipe. After drinking a goblet of mulce, he said, "Good evening to you, my patients, my friends. Let's eat hearty of this great bounty that Arvey has given us."

A patient said, "Tell us something from Arvey's life. Something that happened."

"I'll be glad to. He arrives in New Oleo, Thursday, April 25, 1963. He rents an apartment, then makes a list. His last list. 'Typing! Crystal for watch! Job! Bank account! Mail! Job! Haircut . . . library . . . plug for radio . . . haircut.' For Arvey, job and family were number one. Remember, in those days, good grooming was essential to getting good work, and money wasn't free and edible. Thank you. Let's eat."

The nurse whispered to Moldenke, "All of a sudden he's mellow as a cello."

Ophelia offered a toast. "To Dr. Ferry. The best of the best."

"Hip, hip, hooray," chirped the nurse.

Ferry raised his goblet in acceptance of the toast. "Nurse, were there any latecomers?"

"Yes, Doctor. Moldenke there. He was late."

Ferry lit his pipe again, placed his hands behind his back, and circled the table unsteadily. "Nurse, go get a sergeant. Have this tardy bastard taken to the magistrate."

"Yes, Doctor."

CANDIDATE MONTFAUCON SAT dutifully at the window of his country cottage, his gibnut pistol trained on the winding, stink-water ditch that defined the limit of his property. A band of neutrodyne ruffians had been coming there to drink water. Montfaucon wanted a clear shot. Cranking open his jalousie, he looked out toward the ditch, across a zone of fine white sand and dying sucker weed. He could see the smoke of the neutrodynes' fires and the dust of their ponies.

Three of them rode up to the yard and dismounted. They scaled his wall and went toward the well. Montfaucon's pistol blinked in the sunlight and a single shot was fired. A neutrodyne fell over, wounded in the abdomen. The other two shinnied the fence and fled. Montfaucon went out to examine the downed neut, who was straining to lay a death egg.

"Does it hurt to lay them?" Montfaucon asked.

"Not a bit. It's quite nice. A relief, you know, a compensation for dying. It's all explained in the *Manifesto* . . . I quote, 'There are three universes in the neutrodyne cosmology. One lies in the singularity's future and is dominated by ordinary American matter. Universe two is not our own, but borrowed from the French. It lies in the singularity's past and is dominated by ephemeral material such as ectoplasm. Universe three lies in the spacelike regions of the nanosecond world. It is inhabited by dream figures.'"

"You neuts, do you believe in magic?"

"We do not believe in magic but in Yogic, a marriage of Logic and Yoga. There are three levels of Yogic—the Pomologo, or Botticelli Level, the Porto Venere, or Venus Trap, and the Satchmo, what we call Happy Time, a condition in which the soul sits motionless and all *apparent* life ceases. The idea of cyclical creations, destructions, and great Forgettings is a typical feature of Yogic belief. The culture of Yogic, as it is known from the Settlement Period, is completely *sui generis*, with no trace of celestial influence. Art is the communication of feeling. Science is the communication of measure. Yogic is the communication of the intuitive leap. And what is the intuitive leap? Even expecting tomorrow's sun is such a leap. This is both what Yogic is about and what Yogic has nothing at all to do with."

Loud gurglings came from the neut's abdomen as the last eggs of the batch made their way toward his cloaca, then out into the ample seat of his filthy underdrawers. That finished, the neut expired.

Montfaucon cut open the drawers with his knife and harvested three prize eggs. That evening, after dragging the heavy carcass out where gibnuts would clean it, Montfaucon dined royally on the neut's roasted eggs.

Radio Ratt:

The tenth planet from the sun is named after its discoverer, Leuko Vink. Leuko flies in the cold shadow of distant Neptune, and before the last Forgetting was known as Pumpsylvania. Vink discovered the planet through a handheld telescope given him by the luckless neut astronomer Gold Nose Percival. "Until I found Leuko," Vink says, "I had been constipated for three months. . . . In Indian Apple, Tick Harrison, a Stinker wearing a Humongous costume has been charged with sodomizing a mud duck in Pilchard Park No. 5. The Stinker had rented the costume in Uncle Bob's Monster Shop about 6 P.M. yesterday, then made its way to the park, where it searched for and quickly located a duck with which to have congress. Park rangers spotted Harrison's white body amid the greasewoods, heard the duck's pitiable quacking, and quickly forestalled continuation of the act. . . . A liquid nitrogen suicide has been reported near Bum Bay. Rance Headley, American, was found in a secluded area along N Ditch, sitting upright in the bed of his pedal truck. For some time Headley had been employed by MR Breeding Service. His job was to collect spew from neuts and freeze it with liquid nitrogen, which was kept at 300 degrees below zero in a tank in the truck bed. The sergeant in charge reports that when he arrived at the scene, both valves of the tank were open full and that Headley's lips and tongue were frozen solid. No signs of foul play were detected and loved ones reported no known health problems. . . .

ALONG WITH SEVERAL other settler women, Ophelia waddled across the swing bridge to the old Bum Bay breeding station. Time-stained as it was, its sills and posts rotted, the station still attracted the women's eyes as they approached, particularly the spacious galleries with their elegant cast-iron railings set in heart-shaped cartouches, and their entwined "H" monograms repeated many times along the length.

Out of an open door came a sickly sweet odor. Through a kitchen window the women saw a group of breeder neuts seated at a table, lunching on fungu cakes and roasted locusts. Above them hung a portrait of Arvey, his great blue eyes gazing dreamily over the scene, the collar of his black overcoat raised a bit by a strong Russian wind.

When Ophelia rang the bell, it was the young Vink who answered the door. "Hello, Miss. I remember you. At sea. Aboard the *Titanic*. You ate some of my green gland."

"I can't tell you how luscious it was. Unforgettable."

"I work in the kitchen here. And I do service when I'm needed. Come in, ladies. You all have appointments?" Vink's generously oiled hair seethed with lice and his fiery red beard was peppered with locust legs, wings, and a dry squirt or two of green juice.

DAVID OHLE

The breeders all got up from their lunches, stood before the Arvey portrait, and recited in chorus, "Typing . . . crystal for watch . . . job . . . bank account . . . mail . . . job . . . haircut . . . library . . . plug for radio . . . haircut."

"Make your choices now, ladies," said Vink.

The women went into the refectory to have a closer look. There was some thought that a woman could increase the chances of bearing a female neut by picking a breeder with a well-formed flocculus.

Vink whispered to Ophelia, "I have a good record. Sixty or ninety hundred males, only onety-one or twoty-two females."

Pursuaded by Vink's lilac scent and his pleasant-looking flocculus, she said, "I guess it's you."

"Good choice," Vink said. "*Laissez les bons temps roulez.*" He did an awkward little jig, took Ophelia's arm, and ascended the stairs. "Did you know, ma'am, that warfare in any society is the result of the interaction of protein supply and population density? That's why a diet of fungu and mulce, supplemented with locusts and such, keeps us breeder neuts peaceable and happy. We can be a friend to your people. We can serve your needs in many ways. I'm the first to admit we lack sensibility, but we do have a modicum of pride and a keen sense of smell."

"Talk on," Ophelia said. "I love it."

"There was a time, you know, after my trial for sedition, when I learned to be idle. I wandered about from house to house, asking for crusts and clabber at back windows. I tattled and became a busybody, speaking things I oughtn't. Arrested, I was publicly spanked. Then, in short order, there I was haunting the alleyways again, selling hair to innocent children, spreading gossip like butter. Again arrested, my feet were clubbed with bowling pins and I was set free, barefoot, to roam the icy streets. I fell asleep on a gutter's edge. By morning my feet were frozen and had turned a sickening blue. Even now they are numb, as pale and cold as marble."

"Please, don't stop. More."

"Back in '08 I published a pamphlet treating my revelations having to do with the mysterious kinetics of metamorphic rock. I spoke of my observation, while living in a cardboard and carpet-scrap shack on the open plain west of Bum Bay, that stones were moving, some due north, some south, some indifferently. Gneiss and schist were the worst offenders. Apparently these notions were not taken well among the settlers, who plugged my stovepipe with oily rags. When I started a fire in the potbelly one cool morning the draft reversed and a burning jayhawk flew out the door."

"More, please."

"In a moment. Let's go to a mating room."

After briskly climbing the old stairs, they entered a room furnished with a hair-stuffed pallet on the floor, a rack for hanging clothes, and a small table with washbowl and towel.

Vink faced the wall and Ophelia began undressing. "I wish they hadn't taken away my Vink thinker. It so enhanced every sensation." She lay on the pallet, trying to relax. "Talk to me, to get my egg bag to open."

"Yes ma'am. . . . The simple, two-lobed neutrodyne liver produces a flammable oil in sufficient quantities to make our urine, once denatured, a practicable fuel for lamps and cooking."

"Oh, my."

"After the first Forgetting we gathered outside windows and watched settler families at supper, carefully observing table manners and eating habits. We tipped imaginary cups to our rough, chitinous lips, then applied imaginary napkins. We wanted to know."

She pulled him down on top of her. "Don't stop."

"Awkward and ill-equipped for the purpose, we nevertheless entered public lavatories and attempted to defecate, urinate, and wash ourselves in your fashion—always meeting with failure and humiliation."

"More. I'm still dry."

"Despite having hearts the size of medicine balls, our emotions are skin-deep, signaled only by blushings and palings. It takes a long time for us to recover from light exercise, and digestion is an all day affair."

Vink belched, spraying a yellow mist into Ophelia's face.

"That was good. Don't hesitate to do it again. But talk, talk. I can feel my egg bag opening."

"The neutrodyne life is one of striving without success, limited as we are by the scarcity of circulating blood-oxygen in the body and lacking that subtle lever of oxygen-binding iron hemoglobin wrapped in corpuscles like you have."

"Ahhhhh. Mmmmmm. May I kiss and suck your flocculus?"

Vink parted his beard and presented it, engorged and leaking.

"Give me that and don't stop talking." Ophelia took its hairy end into her mouth. "So sweet. It must be ripe. Go on."

"Some success was achieved in training neutrodynes to sing, to compose limericks for idle entertainment, but I like to play musical instruments, especially the French horn. Music is the fourth material want of the neutrodyne nature, you know. First is food, raiment, then shelter, and finally music. Ratt encourages us to play the French horn, to whistle on the streets, to toot kazoos and reed pipes. Once a year, though, beginning on President Kenny Day, we observe a period we call 'five dark days,' during which we do nothing but lie in the gutters and weep."

Ophelia spat out the flocculus. "I'm almost ready for the *membre*. Just a bit more blather."

"They say neutrodyne sons taste their mother's urine daily, and with added pleasure at the onset of menses. Our son will do that. And often a crossbreed will marry his grandmother. Neutrodynes are absurdly superstitious, too. It was discovered that the moldy *membre* of the Arvey Mummy, stolen by vandals many years ago, was being continually rushed about from camp to camp, village to village, thus circulating haphazardly all over the land in a harmonica box. No sooner was it dropped by one neut than it was caught up by another and hastened on its never-ending journey, bound for no place in particular, but never allowed to rest. A dreadful calamity, it was thought, would befall the neut that let the member halt too long on the premises."

"More. Just a little more. I'm beginning to drip."

"Certain derivatives of human feces are thought to induce dream travel in us by inhibiting the production of a substance that facilitates the transfer of messages along tachyon networks, bundle to bundle. In dreams we have none of the frailties of the body. The dead, though they die, are not dead. The living do not live, though they are alive. In dreams we have no perception of time, and if this property could be retained in the waking state, by whatever means, then time would appear as eternity. We would live forever. I further postulate that, while most of eternity is compressed into a moment, in dreams, infinite space is traversed more swiftly than by real thought."

"I'm ready for the *membre virile*," Ophelia said.

Vink unbuckled his heavy, woven-hair trousers and let them fall to the floor. His two-shafted mating *membre* stiffened.

"May I touch them?"

"As you wish."

Ophelia wrapped a hand around each of the *membres*, both hard as flint and uncomfortably warm.

"May I oil them?"

"*Mais oui.*"

A bottle of mummy oil lay handy on a window sill. She poured a goodly amount in her palm and applied it first to the upper shaft, then the lower. "They say you get no pleasure from sexing with us. And we get so much."

"What's never there is never missed, or mourned. It's a matter of balance and a cultural imperative."

"Talk to me more."

"Back in Indiana, before the last Forgetting, trams and trolley cars had become obsolete. The public began to travel by pedal bus. More and more, cities required passengers to have the exact change when boarding—or 'tokens.'"

"Tokens? What are tokens?"

"Small disks, coinlike. Similar to the French *jeton.* These could be purchased in advance. For some years, drivers had the double job of making change at the same time they were operating their monster buses through headlong traffic. The new exact-change rule eased the driver's load, speeded service for everyone, and reduced the number of robberies that took place when the driver was in possession of so much money. And then . . . to make a long story short, edible paper made its debut, and nothing was ever the same again."

"Enter me now. They're oiled and I'm ready."

When the *membres* entered and began their measured, repetitive thrusting, Ophelia cried out in pain, then pleasure. She felt the *membres* swell, heard the bubbling of Vink's protracted lilac-scented spewing, the milk-white fluid so abundant it poured out of her, mixed with her blood, soaking the pallet and wetting half the floor.

"It feels like I've swallowed a bucket of dough," she said.

"We thank you for your kind help," Vink said, giving her ten guida. The edible, glutinous note smelled slightly of ammonia and stale ink. It had been handled, rolled, folded, crushed, and thumbed long enough to give it the feel of flesh itself. "Payment will be in full should you bear a male. That will come when you register at the Rattery. If it's a female, you know what to do."

"Yes, I know."

THIS TIME MOLDENKE faced Magistrate Yodel, known for his leniency and sleepy demeanor.

"Moldenke . . . Moldenke . . . Moldenke. Is that a last name or a first?"

"A last, sir. My first was lost in the last Forgetting."

"Aha. So many lost so much. . . . What's the charge here, Sergeant?"

The sergeant in charge nudged Moldenke closer to the bench. "Late for dinner, Magistrate."

Yodel cupped his hand behind his ear. "What's that clicking I hear? Nevermind, I see the bulge. And I know the whole story. You went to Ferry for deformation."

"I went in for a bad implant, a flocculus, and a case of worms."

"What sort of implant?"

"Hearts. One original, three sheep. Pre-Forgetting. Burnheart's early work. They were old, going bad. Ferry used pig this time. French pig."

"And talked you into new testes? Told you the worms had descended and ravaged your old ones?"

"Yes."

"And these testes . . . also French pig by any chance?"

"He was running a special."

"He's always running a special on them. And they're not pig, my lad, they're from old breeder neuts. And don't ask me where that heart came from, although I've heard reports he's keeping young Stinkers in his garage. I wouldn't be surprised if that's where he harvests them. He's a liar and a fraud, the Arvian shit that he is. If he ever comes before me, I'll throw a book at him. Probably *The Grassy Knoll*. . . . Do you have a waiver, Moldenke?"

"He has no waiver, Magistrate," said the sergeant.

"Then give him one. Give him two or three. Case dismissed."

Yodel retired to his chambers yawning.

"He'll sleep the afternoon away is what he'll do," the sergeant said. "And look at this line of defendants." He gave Moldenke three waivers, then took one back. "One for this offense and two to go."

THE NEXT MORNING Moldenke took a pedal cab to the Squat 'n' Gobble, where he ordered mulce and gland.

"Gland's out of season," the neut gal said. "What about some gibnut soup?"

"Soup it is. And a mulce with phosphate."

"Someone was in here asking about you. Ophelia something."

"Ophelia, of course."

"What a pair of dugs she has."

"Ferry's work. What did she say?"

"To tell you goodbye for awhile. She's going to Valdosta."

"What's the charge this time?"

"Conspiracy to kill the president."

"Pity. What's the hair situation these days? Lawful? Available?"

"Here comes a newsboy. He'll sell you a smoke." She waved to the one-legged newsboy, pointing to Moldenke and touching her fingers to her lips in a smoking gesture. "Over here! This American."

The newsboy hopped over to Moldenke. "Primo. Onety-zil and ten."

"Quite pricey, *non*?"

"Believe me, sir. This is the best. The saffron of hair. Aged in polar ice a thousand years, ever since the Age of Sinatra."

Moldenke bought ten pre-rolls and a box of Shur-Strike matches.

The newsboy placed an *Observer* on the countertop. "How about a paper? This thing is stuffed with news. Read it and weep. 'Flocculus Rates Skyrocket! *Titanic* Raised! Anti-Ratt Underground Probed. Forgetting Set for Blossom-5.'"

"No, thanks. Allergic to the ink."

"Lots of new statutes you need to know about. They're all in here. First copy's free."

"All right. Leave it."

"You want more smoke, you know where to find it. I'm around. Name's Jack Dawes."

Moldenke lit up a smoke and held the paper at arm's length. The first headline that came into view, blurred and indistinct, was '*Titanic* Raised. Three dead, six hurt, eleven will hang.' Squinting and blinking, he began reading the article:

> A sea burial nightmare ended today. "Fast, she sank, once the Forgetting took hold," said one survivor. "We fought fiercely for the airy cabin we have occupied since the teens of this century.

Even desperate fist-bangings against our door would not move us to sacrifice the space designed to save our girl baby, ourselves, and our cockatiel, Virginia.

"Drifting bottomward for hours, we heard the steady thunk of the air compressor in our closet, preserving us. A bubble in the blood-stream of the chilled Atlantic is all we were. We ate squid tentacles, whale's eyes, the meat of the plesiosaur. We relished the tasty brain of the por-poise, though we convulsed with shame with every swallow.

"As the years brought the soldiers of time against us, our bodies glowed within and talk turned to adopting abyssal fish as gods.

"We believed ourselves alone until the day we began to receive the transmissions of Radio Ratt, initiating slight flickers of our blubber lamp, informing us in a simple, informational way that existence without contradiction is unthinkable. He knows that if you ever reach a state of har-mony within yourself, he cannot hope to stand against your City of Mind, your *synedrium*, your species."

Before Moldenke could finish the article, and perhaps learn if Udo was among the survivors, Del Piombo entered the Squat. Moldenke folded the *Observer* and pushed it to the very edge of the counter. Still, his eyes burned and his cheeks tingled.

"Piombo? You?"

"Yes, me. And with exciting news. We're all uniting under Montfaucon, even the neuts. And now the Arvians are on the bandwagon. Finally, a power center has developed." He handed Moldenke a weighty object wrapped in brown, edible paper. "This device was made by inventor Vink. He's come over to our side. He says it will fire an explosive projectile far enough and with enough force to puncture the skin of Ratt's balloon and ignite the gas. At rallies, he sits right under it. The force of the explosion will kill him. If not, the flames will."

"And I'm the one to . . . and my part in this is . . . to burst the balloon?"

"Not you. Someone else. Someone more specialized. When the time comes, you will give him the device."

"I am obliged, Mr. Piombo, to ask . . . in light of the coming Forgetting . . . why bother killing Ratt, if all memory of him is soon to be lost and gone forever?"

Piombo gave the question serious thought. "I'll tell you what Montfaucon says, in the strictest privacy. Coded transmissions from Radio Ratt bring on the Forgettings. On a day-to-day basis, they prepare us for that eventuality. It's a very mysterious process, the radio news delicately interwoven with the daily papers. Strings of well-chosen words, vocal intonation, manipulations of the amplitude, every sort of audio magic. Whenever he wants the slate of his horrors wiped clean, he merely pulls a switch and turns a knob. You kill Ratt, topple his transmitters, you end the Forgettings."

"I see," Moldenke said.

"Spread the word. Doubt everything you see or hear until further notice."

"I thought as much."

"Give up your room at the Adolphus. Return to the mansion. Keep the device there. We want you located closer to Dilly Plaza. Plans have a way of changing and changing quickly."

GERALD HITLER AWAKENED in terror from a fretful sleep. His head worms, inactive much of the winter, had begun to stir from their torpor. He found at least a half-dozen crawling on his pillow, already growing little legs and leaving circuitous trails of silvery slime. Now his thinking would be muddied for the duration of the summer months.

Pulling on his jumpsuit, he wiped away the mold that had accumulated on his clogs overnight, then stepped unsteadily into them. He made himself a light breakfast of dried green gland, some mulce, and a johnnycake. Then, as he did every morning, he smoked a bowl of hair, moved his bowels, and placed his slop pot outside the door for collection. After these rituals were over, he headed for the pedal bus stop, planning to attend a vivisection. Being commonplace, vivisections would not ordinarily attract the paper's attention, but this one was being performed by the perennial newsmaker Agnes Moldenke.

Her days at Valdosta had ended when she was pardoned by Ratt moments after the long-delayed news of her incarceration reached him. Home again, settled in with Moldenke at her mansion, she had taken up the practice of vivisection, principally as a form of distraction and amusement, and enlisted Moldenke's assistance in exchange for room and board.

Hilter's bus ride was uneventful until the bus reached the corner of N Ditch and Wallow Street. There, a neutrodyne passenger, jumping off in a fit of haste, caught his coat on a protruding piece of iron and was dragged over a distance of one hundred feet before the driver was attracted by the gasps of pedestrians and disengaged the pedal chain.

By the time the bus coasted to a stop, the neut's carcass and clothing had tangled in gearwork. The conductor got out to assess the situation, then came back to say, "It's impossible to continue until we undo that smelly mess and sponge the undercarriage with a disinfecting agent. So get out there and stretch those legs."

As the driver and the conductor oversaw the cleaning operation, Hilter crossed the street and went into the Rattery to see the latest exhibits, including that of Mrs. Moldenke's latest work.

"A remarkable experience," he would later write in the *Observer*. "A mountainscape of liver paste, whole battalions of wurst soldiers ready to march up green gland hill and down again. You will see Punch and Judy made of head cheese, two rollicksome figures that jibe at each other across the mincemeat gulch, while a group of death egg warriors gives the viewer a strange feeling of unity and power."

In the Rattery's neutrodyne wing, a troupe of enthusiastic neuts were performing their latest shadow plays by holding images made of camphor bark at the ends of sticks and manipulating them in front of a bright fusel-oil lamp.

The troupe's director, acting as docent, said, "We have adapted to the uses of our theater some of the dramas of Sincay Baxter and we have also designed the tableaux, which illustrate the progress of the *dramattes*."

The first *dramatte* of the matinée, projected onto a muslin sheet, depicted Arvey asleep in a jail cell. Paper dreams—of serpents, worms, and spiders—fluttered upward and away from his tortured head.

The lamp then dimmed and the tableau darkened. The second part of the *dramatte* began with a parade of shadow figures bringing food to the condemned Arvey, who gulped it down in great quantities and fattened grossly as larger and larger cutouts were placed before the lamp.

The docent said, "It is time for the execution."

A neutrodyne jailer entered the cell, dragged the bloated Arvey to the gallows, and placed a rope around his neck.

"Have you any final words?" the executioner asked.

"I didn't shoot anybody," was the reply. As the knot slid home, Arvey spat in the hangman's face. When he dropped to the end of the rope, Arvey's head came off, falling at a distance from the body.

"This *dramatte* was called 'Death of the Devil,'" said the docent.

Hilter left a guida in the bucket provided and moved on to see the green gland collection. The glands were arrayed under glass in all phases of their behavior range: enlarged, pulsating, retracted, quiescent, fruiting, and edible. A sheet of text explained the nature of the neutrodyne organ.

The green gland has had a long history of study, often yielding contradictory evidence. Theories have been proposed to account for its modifications. Whatever the phylogenetic or ontogenetic significance, it is known to be formed by invaginations of the head capsule in utero. At birth, the green gland begins its lifelong journey through the neutrodyne body, traveling with a will of its own. At death, it is expelled in the form of an egg from the most convenient orifice, most often the anus.

Before returning to the bus, Hilter took in the first showing of the fully restored Arvey. When he reached the mezzanine, there were small groups of people standing at a balcony, chatting softly, sipping mulce, and eating cubes of hardened fungu. Everyone was looking down at the main parlor, where the restored Arvey rested on a granite catafalque, a steady line of visitors filing past. Some threw guida, which landed in a sand-filled trough that ran around the base of the catafalque.

"It's quite a source of revenue for the Ratt Administration," one of the visitors said to Hilter. "It can walk now, for short periods. They tell me it walked up and down the mezzanine stairs this morning. It was talking a minute ago, too. Throw in some guida and ask it something."

Hilter donated a few guida and thought for a moment before asking, "Is it true, that you shot Kenny dead?"

The heels of Arvey's black Russian shoes snapped together with a dull *clack* and he spoke in a clear, strong voice. "I didn't shoot anybody. I had a daughter named June. When Marina was undergoing painful lactation, I offered to suckle her breasts to keep them from swelling with milk."

A custodian drew a cloth over the head. "No more questions, please. He's very tired and weak."

Hilter boarded the bus again and in a short time arrived at Mrs. Moldenke's mansion. For her part, she had been up early that morning, douching, tending her hair, breakfasting on cold mulce custard, then, to disguise herself as a Persian Gypsy, she put on a blue blouse flowered with yellow roses, black satin trousers, a dark red skirt reaching to her knees, and a tight-fitting, open-collar shift. Finally, she lined her satchel with cheesecloth and filled the chloroform bottle right to the top. "I'm going to get a specimen," she said to Moldenke. "While I'm gone, please get the dais ready and set out the chairs."

"How many chairs, Mother?"

"Oh, a dozen I'd say. A small group of very close friends and Gerald Hilter of the *Observer*. Make sure my things are ready . . . the amber petroleum wax, the benzoin, the nuclidine, the quinuclidinyl, the carbolic, the lithia, the sack of phosphate, and don't forget the cochineal. I suspect I'll be in a rather . . . red . . . mood tonight."

"As you say, Mother."

It was not like her to venture out on such a gnatty, humid morning. In fact, during the warm months she seldom left her dais. It was there that she prayed, ate, slept, practiced her art, attended to her widespread affairs, and received her many visitors.

This dais was as large as a good-sized room but raised six feet above the ground and situated at the east end of the courtyard. Every second day the white linen covering of the dais was removed. The small square of silk on which Mrs. Moldenke sat, cross-legged, to work with her specimens was changed three times a day.

Mrs. Moldenke pedaled her little car to the Eastside Historic Area. Somewhat disoriented, she asked a neutrodyne roasting locusts in a temple vestibule for directions to the Squat 'n' Gobble.

"You can walk there from here. Go through the Plaza, past the latrine, then follow the smell of sour mulce."

"Thank you for the courtesy, neut."

As she approached the public latrine, Mrs. Moldenke's abdomen growled and gave notice, as if it could see. She went in and sat with others on a wooden platform built high above a running trench. As it was now unlawful to converse, or read while toileting, everyone silently went about their business, attentively listening to the splash of urine and the *kerflop* of excrement resounding in the trench below.

At the Squat 'n' Gobble, she found Ophelia Balls waiting at the rear entrance, a swirling army of sawflies gathered around her head.

"Mrs. Moldenke?"

"Too bad we meet under these regrettable circumstances."

"Bad luck, I suppose."

"Bad luck? I don't think so, Ophelia. In nine cases out of ten, bad luck is the result of bad company. You voluntarily sexed with a neutrodyne. You knew the consequences for a female birth."

Ophelia shrugged and turned toward the darker shadows.

They went into the Squat and ordered mulces. Mrs. Moldenke said, "I presume you wish to surrender your little offspring to me for use in my vivisection practice?"

"I do. I've been keeping it in a tub of salted gelatin, according to sanitary law."

"Good, good."

"I didn't even know she was *in* me. I woke up in the middle of the night, my dugs full of mulce to the bursting point, and there she was, in the bed, cuddled up to me, sleeping. My dugs hurt terribly unless I let her nurse for hours on end. The sharp teeth cut me and I bled."

"My sympathies, dearie. Trying to raise crossbreeds can be trying."

"As soon as she was freed in my room, she began defying me, hair bristling, arrogant with fighting spirit. She pitted her will against mine, running up and down the curtains, finding ingenious ways of going from one end of the room to the other without touching the floor. Gradually she began to accept me as a movable fixture and a source of no disturbance. But she was always nervously alert, and when she sunbathed on the windowsill she sat in a tense, tight ball, singing ditties for hours in a shrill monotone. I fixed a place for her with rubber pillows and raffia mats at one end of my mattress."

"Yes, well, that's very sweet."

"And then that red wattle appeared beneath her chin and added the final touch to her odd little face. She liked it when I took hold of her wattle and pulled it. Then she grew a stubby, gray beard and a silken moustache, followed by a growth of brownish fur on the rest of her head. And she began to give off the scent of rotting hay. Even so, I have a mother's affection for her. I've named her Little Angelina Vink."

"Where is the thing now?"

"Outside, in the alley."

"I assure you I'll give her all the best treatments."

Leaving Ophelia in tears, Mrs. Moldenke went into the alley and knelt beside the tub of gelatin, carefully lifting out the little half-neut and placing her inside the satchel. A muffled voice came through the slightly opened zipper. "Hey, you look slick. Are you Persian? Will you be my mother?"

"I've got the specimen," she told Moldenke on arriving home. "Look after it while I wash myself and get my instruments." She set the satchel on the dais and crossed the courtyard toward the bathhouse.

As other guests arrived and found their places, Moldenke busied himself changing linens, setting out plenty of cotton and drain pans. Likewise, he made sure there were ample supplies of fungu, roots, and mulce for the guests. Hilter sat in the rearmost seat and took careful notes.

Little Angelina, feigning sleep, could be heard snoring in the satchel. When Moldenke had finished his duties, he opened the satchel and she spoke to him. "Say . . . where is my daddy? Will you be my daddy?" There were hushed chuckles among the guests.

"Likely not," Moldenke said, lifting her out of the satchel. "Now, you hurry and undress. It's time to have your chloroform. Look, here comes Mrs. Moldenke. Lie back. Put your head on this little pillow. Take a whiff now."

Mrs. Moldenke, wearing jester's dress of green velvet, with bells on her feet and castanets on her hands, performed a saraband before the guests, then prepared her instruments. Little Angelina took her hand and kissed it, saying, "Allow me to spend my last breath on kissing the hand of the inventor of edible money."

Mrs. Moldenke raised the wick of her fusel-oil lamp and unwrapped a set of fine, steel instruments from an oil-damp cloth. "The moon is fat and blue tonight," she said. "An excellent evening for this kind of art. Now, where did I put that quinuclidinyl and that number-four mallet?"

When the chloroform had been applied, Mrs. Moldenke began the vivisection by breaching the cloacal opening and drawing out the sweetbreads with a suction bulb. "Ah, the cloaca," Mrs. Moldenke said. "Here we have a remarkable cavity. Its name derives from that of an ancient sewer, or privy. It is the common bucket into which the intestinal, urinary, and generative canals open . . . in birds, reptiles, amphibians, many fishes, certain mammals, and neutrodynes."

The diaphragm was then cut, to allow removal of the air bladder and the heart, which were packed in wet sawdust.

"Art is done, life's begun," Mrs. Moldenke said. "I have what I want. Take care of the husk." She put the eggs and the sweetbreads into a jar of brine.

Moldenke wrapped Little Angelina's husk in muslin and flung it into a small, *poudrette*-fueled incinerator, where a hot, coppery flame consumed all traces. As he did so, the guests engaged in lively discussions about Mrs. Moldenke's performance, finished up all the mulce, and left.

It was time to put away the instruments and mop the dais. As Moldenke concluded these chores, there were footsteps along the outer wall, then a knock at the courtyard's greasewood gate. "I'm afraid the show is over," he said. "Come back another time."

A voice from the other side of the gate spoke softly, dryly. "Look up there," it whispered. "In the western sky." It was a voice Moldenke had heard before.

Rising above the Zeus Bologna plant and moving in the direction of the Rattery was the Michael Ratt balloon. It would soon be over Dilly Plaza.

"Get me the device," said the voice. "Do not open the gate. Do not look at me. Things will go easier for you that way." He'd heard the voice before but had forgotten where or when or whose it was.

Going to his room, Moldenke took the device from his closet, unwrapped it, wiped away the sticky residue of the edible paper, and made certain the explosive cartridge was in a position to fire when the trigger mechanism was engaged.

As he passed his mother's door on the way out, she called him in to say, "I sense something in the air. A premonition. A Forgetting is very close. You should make out your list of things to remember."

"Yes, Mother. That could very well be, and I will."

"Good night, now, my dear. Be a good boy, and prepare for tomorrow."

"Yes, Mother," he said. "I will."

Moldenke jogged across the courtyard and held the weapon above the gate. It was quickly snatched from his grasp and there were retreating footsteps along the banquette wall. Opening the gate slightly, he managed a brief glance at the figure, a small man in a rumpled, ill-fitting overcoat and oversize black shoes, who stopped, turned, and met Moldenke's gaze. Pinched, wasp-like, his face showed no expression. He tapped his watch with a long, yellow finger-nail. "I'm late for my appointment with the President," he said, clicking his heels and turning up Arden Boulevard. Moldenke kept an eye on the man until he was lost in the crowd of revelers headed for Dilly Plaza.

Returning to the house, he entered his mother's room and sat on her plush vanity chair. She was sleeping deeply and snoring. "I've gotten myself entangled in something, Mother. I don't think it will end very well."

The snoring stopped. Turning like an armature under the coverlet, Mrs. Moldenke rolled over. "Goodnight, dear. Nothing to worry about. Go to bed. Go. Go." She fell back to sleep and the snoring began.

Too anxious to sleep, Moldenke took a pedal cab to the Squat 'n' Gobble, passing Dilly Plaza on the way. It was a breezy night and the Ratt balloon, tethered above the grand-stand, twisted erratically. He paused awhile to watch, until a sergeant came along.

"What's so amusing about the balloon, friend?"

"Nothing, really. Just having a look. On my way to the Squat."

"Get going, then. It's all-you-can-eat plesio tonight. But they close in a few minutes."

"Oh, good. Very good."

The Squat's dinner crowd was thinning and Moldenke quickly found an empty stool.

"The plesio platter, please."

"Fresh out," the fry cook said. "All we got left this time of night are boiled roots."

"Nevermind. Just a mug of mulce then."

"It's a little sour, and we ran out of phosphate."

"All right. A mug of the sour mulce."

"The mulce wagons aren't making deliveries tonight. The drivers are all at the rally."

Someone behind Moldenke squeezed his shoulder, then sat next to him.

"Moldenke."

"Piombo."

"How goes it?"

"Well enough, I guess."

"He came for the device?"

"Yes."

"Then it'll all be over for Ratt very soon."

The Squat suddenly brightened as the sky lit up, followed by a muffled concussion that shattered the windows and tumbled cookware from the shelves. Sounds of panic and confusion entered through the broken glass, along with a pulse of hot, dry air.

"Finally, the beast is dead," Piombo said. "It's every man for himself."

THE FOLLOWING DAY Moldenke was arrested and charged with killing Ratt and three of his attendants by firing an incendiary device at the Michael Ratt balloon, causing it to explode with deadly force.

"For killing the President," said Magistrate Yerkimer, "and three of his honored attendants, you shall soon plunge into that uncertain darkness by hanging. Have you anything to say?"

"Yes. I have a waiver."

"Only one?"

"Two. I have two."

"This is clearly a three-waiver case. However, credit is allowed for the two you have. That considered, I sentence you to, oh, about twoty-three years at Valdosta."

"Sergeant, arrange a seat for him on the next orbigator going there."

"Thank you, sir, for showing such mercy."

"You're welcome, son. Off you go, now. Sergeant, arrest someone important. Someone the people love and honor. We'll hang them at sunrise tomorrow. It will be open to the public."

Radio Montfaucon:
The new President outlined his vision today in a communiqué from his French Sewer operations office. The principal goal of the Montfaucon administration, the communiqué reveals, is to adopt the principle goal of the previous administration. "We'll keep all the old ways intact," Montfaucon is quoted as saying, "with just a few modifications." Details of the modifications will be announced at a later time. . . . Meanwhile, the French prodigist Archille Topinard died today in a Bloomberg squat after tucking into a large plate of gibnut liver and choking. A physician sitting at the next table ran to help, but Topinard fell forward with a moan, gasping for breath. It was reported that the famous prodigist, in despair after the death of his giant, Indole, had determined to eat himself to death. By noon he had consumed ten bowls of green gland soup, two pounds of roots, a whole grasshopper pie, and seven pitchers of fermented mulce. . . . In New Oleo, inventor Vink has overseen the construction of a prototype Forgetting shelter. Building plans for the shelter will soon to be available to the public, Vink says, but cautions that in any Forgetting of long duration, the dreadful monotony of the shelter can be a danger in itself and lead to violent outbreaks of temper and sometimes to murderous acts.

ON HIS WAY to the orbigator station, Moldenke passed the Sinatra Home for Wayward Neutrodynes. A female was perched on the stoop with a sign that said, I Read Minds. Her head was pie-like, presenting a broad face but a narrow profile. As it turned toward him, he saw less and less of it, until it was but a slice. She was licking the last of the mulce from a gourd and giving off an odor so sickly sweet Moldenke looked down to see if he had stepped on a stinkbug.

"Say, American, you look slick. I'll make you an offer. If I guess your name, you be my sponsor and take me to Valdosta with you."

"What makes you think I'm going to Valdosta?"

The neut pointed a damp finger at her sign. "Then name guessing should be easy, shouldn't it?"

"Yes. But you'll never guess the first."

"It's there, but illegible, in a fog, forgotten I'd say. Give me a minute. Let's have a ciggie while I cogitate. You carrying?"

Moldenke gave her one of the hundred Hairloom ready-rolls he was taking to Valdosta, which she ate, then he lit one for himself. He could hear the orbigator's engines turning and its horns sounding incessantly. The noise echoed among the empty, sealed buildings of the historic area.

"I'm in a bit of a rush, you know. If I miss my flight they'll probably have me beheaded."

"It's coming, the name."

"Wasted effort. I lost it in the last Forgetting. This is pure confabulation."

"It's Baxter. . . . Baxter Sincay Moldenke."

"Ridiculous. Baxter Sincay was that famous settler poet."

"Who lost his last name in the Forgetting of '66. Don't you remember? You must have been him. You forgot. Come on, Baxter, take me to Valdosta."

"I don't believe you. You pulled that name out of thin air. And why would you want to go to Valdosta? Taking neuts there can get me into trouble."

"Not any more. Don't you read the papers? Montfaucon's in office. Valdosta's the place for neuts to be right now. All I need is a sponsor. I can put the squeeze on the Americans there, fleece them out of their guida with my guessing game. I'll cut you in for half. You shill for me. I do the tricks. And yes, you can sex with me whenever you want. And think about mulcing season, right around the corner. My dugs'll fill up and you can have all you can drink. My name's Melody."

Moldenke's Stinker heart pumped vigorously and he felt the weight and warmth of his new scrotal sack between chilled legs. "Pack up your sign, gal. I'll sponsor you."

"Rock 'n' roll," Melody said.

Moldenke had never heard the expression. "What is rock and roll?"

"Sorry. That's pre-Forgetting, Sinatra-Age stuff. You wouldn't remember."

A steward collected tickets as passengers stepped off the gangway. "Welcome aboard the *Noctule*. We'll be underway in exactly an hour or two. Have a cocktail in the Arvey Room while you wait. No reading or spitting. We arrive in Valdosta next week sometime."

"We're on the way to something big," Melody said, choosing a table with a good view of the surrounding landscape. "Rock 'n' roll, let's get a load on."

Moldenke ordered a pitcher of fermented mulce and fired up a ciggie. "I have a condition," he said. "Sudden electrical discharges from the sacrum. My legs bend. Once and awhile I have to kneel. I know how excitable neut gals can be, so I wanted to warn you."

"You've been to see Ferry, haven't you? You're carrying a big pair, now, aren't you? Feeling your oats, as they used to say. Now that excites me."

"You can tell? Do they show?"

She stuffed a finger in her nose. "By the smell, don't you know."

A crowd of rowdy Indianians were seated at a nearby table, singing, "Artificial respiration could have saved my Clementine, da da da da, da da da da, da da da da, da da da."

A dance instructor led a group of Stinkers onto the floor, accompanied musically by the Chatterjees, a mellophone trio doing a high-strung version of "Mood Indigo." The instructor cued the Stinkers with a harsh tone: "Shuffle! Jump! Toe! Shuffle! Jump! Toe! Flap! Ball change! Flap! Ball change!"

One of the Indianians leaned toward Moldenke. "I have two things to tell you. One, when you get to Valdosta, be sure to visit the area east of the Great Tar Pit, recently settled by the Chinese, and eat at the Palacia Oriental. Prices are steep but they fry their green gland with artistry."

"There were two things," Moldenke said.

"The second thing is, and take it as advice and counsel from a fellow American, the sergeant will be coming around soon and he won't like you buddying up with a neut gal, and most particularly right here in the Arvey Room. Don't you read the papers? It was Montfaucon's first directive when he took office. If I were you, I'd ditch that thing right now."

"This can't be construed as buddying. We have a perfectly legitimate business arrangement."

"You can't say I didn't try to warn you," the Indianian said. "Here comes the heat."

The sergeant entered the Arvey Room followed by a squadron of mates and attendants and went from table to table shaking hands and saying, "Please, shake the hand that shook the hand of the late, adorable Michael Ratt."

But when he stopped at Moldenke's table, his hand was not extended for shaking. "Is that man 'buddying' with you, neut?"

"You think I'd get cozy with a bounder like him?" Melody said. "Not on your life, partner."

The sergeant nodded toward the Indianians. "Any incriminations from over there?"

One of them offered a synopsis: "We were just sitting here, singing, smoking, drinking, minding our own business, and then those two came along. We smelled that sweet musk neuts give off when they're in the mood for mating. We could also detect a strange scent coming from him, too. Right away we knew."

"Are you saying that your every instinct tells you that this pair is contemplating having, or have had, sexual congress?"

"Yessir," the group chorused.

"Thank you. You've performed an important service." The twisted and waxed tips of the sergeant's mustache brushed the sides of his nose when he spoke, causing his eyelids to flutter.

Melody found this effect comical and giggled uncontrollably at the very moment the *Noctule* lifted away from its moorings at a sharp angle. Pitchers of mulce slid from tables and made a slippery mess on the dance floor. The Stinker dancers slipped to the floor one by one with dull, airy thuds and slid around like mud ducks on a frozen lake.

The sergeant spread his feet apart to keep his balance. "So, you find humor in all this, do you? Well, then, with the authority vested in me as chief sergeant on this vessel, I pronounce you man and wife, and, I sentence you both to a lifetime of civil death. Let me see waivers if you have them."

"I don't," Moldenke said.

"Looks like we're hitched, my darling, all legal and everything," Melody said.

The sergeant and his entourage returned to their quarters, the Indianians resumed their singing, and the Chatterjees took five.

Moldenke lit a pre-roll and poured himself another mulce.

"Rock and roll," he said, without joy, "everything's in balance at last."

Radio Montfaucon:
Remarkable illuminations were observed in Bum Bay's northern heavens on Friday and Saturday nights. The bright, diffused white and yellow lights continued through the night and faded at daybreak. President Montfaucon has postulated that the phenomenon may be connected to the onset of another Great Forgetting. He mentioned a similar occurrence back in the foggy last months of Zero Nine, which immediately preceded the disastrous Forgetting of Zero Ten. "Post hoc ergo propter hoc," said the President. "I believe in that principle with all my heart and soul, and it will be the guiding light of my administration." Reports from New Oleo, Indian Apple, and settlements in the Fertile Crescent tell of the same lights being visible in those places. The President also said, "Let these lights be a warning. Make a list of things to remember."

FROM HER CELL the night of Blossom-4, Mrs. Moldenke could see a portion of the rickety, well-used gallows through an oval window in the basement lockup of the Rattery. A sergeant stood idly by as the neuts worked, looking up at a blue moon. Giving thought to her last words, she decided to use the subtitle of her *Book of Surprises*: "Eventually, Why

Not Now?" She passed the night watching a small squad of mulcing neuts braid two ropes, one of which would end her life in the morning. The other rope was for Del Piombo, sentenced by Yerkimer to hang, not for killing the President, but for counterfeiting edible money.

Just after dawn they were taken to the gallows by pedal cart.

"Hurry and hang me," Piombo said, kicking off his clogs. "I'm ready to take the plunge and these are my last words. Life, death, what's the difference? Two sawflies on a picket fence. Every now and then they fly up and change places."

"Good morning, Del," Mrs. Moldenke said. "I suppose we'll meet again aboard the *Titanic*."

"See you in the bistro."

The sergeant said, "Come on, then, old girl, step into that little red circle, right next to Piombo. Anything to say? Last words?"

"I did have, but I've forgotten them. It doesn't matter."

The condemned's hands were tied securely behind their backs and shrouds placed over their heads. When the sergeant nodded, the hangman pulled the lever and, though both were dropped the prescribed distance and Piombo succumbed very quickly, Mrs. Moldenke's neck failed to break. She struggled violently for release.

Among the onlookers was Gerald Hilter. Smoking hair, his pocket stuffed with waivers, he wondered how he would couch this story for tomorrow's edition. Would it be, "Hangings Popular as Montfaucon Takes Office" or, the more succinct, "Moldenke Hanging Badly Botched"?

The sergeant ordered two husky Stinkers to suspend themselves from Mrs. Moldenke's legs until it was thought she was dead. When she stopped moving, the crowd dispersed and the Stinkers lay down to rest.

David Ohle's first novel, *Motorman*, was published by Knopf in 1972 and will be reprinted by 3rd Bed in June 2004. His short fiction has appeared in *Harper's*, *Esquire*, the *Paris Review*, and elsewhere. He compiled and edited *Cursed From Birth: The Short Unhappy Life of William S. Burroughs, Jr.*, published by Grove-Atlantic in 2002. A native of New Orleans, Ohle now lives in Lawrence, Kansas, and teaches at the University of Kansas. His last name rhymes with "holy."